MIDAS TOUCH 2

MASTERPIECE

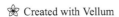 Created with Vellum

SUBSCRIBE

Interested in keeping up with more releases from S.Yvonne
Presents? To be notified first on upcoming releases, exclusive
sneak peaks, and contest to win prizes. Please subscribe to
her mailing list: https://bit.ly/3jKoNbB

SUBSCRIBE

SYNOPSIS

The finale is here, locked and loaded! Relationships have started, while some will end. Lives are bound to be lost in the name of deception and deceit. Midas is a man who doesn't like to show emotions, but when his mother is caught in the crossfire of greed and jealousy, his patience is tested. The entire crew is back with their very own list of problems, as so many secrets are revealed and answered in this final installment. Midas isn't the only one with the Midas Touch for every and anything.

TRIGGER WARNING!!!!!

This book contains content that some may find disturbing!

HISTORI

I watched Daness suck my dick with the right amount of pressure. She sucked so good that my toes were cramping from clenching tight every single time she decided to include my balls into her mouth. Her head was so good that I felt dizzy, and my breath got caught in my throat as I watched Lee get behind her with a strap on dildo.

Lee acted like the dildo was a real dick, as she fake stroked it like she was getting it hard, then tapped it on Daness' pretty, round, brown ass then entered her slowly. She stroked in and out as Daness went up and down on my dick with her warm, wet mouth. The room was filled with sounds of Daness' wet pussy making disrespectful sounds on Lee's strap on dick.

She made gargling sounds and choked a little as she went down to the base of my dick, then came back up, swirling her tongue around the tip.

"Got damn, I hate that I have to kill you bitches." I mumbled under my breath. There was no love, but I couldn't deny the sexual connection that I felt with them. They were nasty as fuck and with the business when it came time for them to put in whatever work I asked of them.

I had to kill them because keeping them alive could potentially fuck me over. They wanted more and more money for some shit that they didn't complete years ago, and that was Midas. Midas dying would have been something perfect for me. I could've easily stepped into my power with no problem.

I wasn't hurting for bread, but I still hadn't touched a million dollars yet. It didn't matter how many hoes I recruited or put on the track to walk until their feet bled out. They cost me money while they gave me money, especially my high paid hoes. I constantly had to get their hair, nails, and feet done. I couldn't put them all under the same roof, so I bought other properties to keep my high paid hoes separated from the street walking hoes.

I expanded to Vegas and that's where I currently am. Midas wouldn't be able to track me down or try some funny shit. This house wasn't in my name, all of my properties were secretly in one of my hoes name.

"Just like that bitch, suck the nut out of my shit." I thrust upward into Daness' mouth as she moaned loudly from the hard back shots that Lee was giving her. I could feel my nut rising and just the thought of being so close to making a couple of millions off of kidnapping Ms. Wellington's stupid ass had me ready to bust a couple of nuts.

"Oh shit!" Daness' nasty ass licked on my gooch and squeezed my dick tightly, stroking it up and down just as my nut started to spurt out. I reached underneath me for my gun but stopped when Lee pulled out of Daness and crawled over to me on her knees.

Her sexy ass dark skin complexion glowed as I eyed her perky breast bouncing with each movement she made. I admired her curvy figure, the arch in her spine was cold as hell, her ass was fat, and just the sight of Lee had me bricking right back up. Daness laid on her back, opening her legs she played with her pussy as Lee licked up and down my shaft. She licked around my pelvis then came up to my stomach placing soft pecks until she reached my nipples. Soon as she bit down on my left nipple, I grunted as my dick started to ache. A small breathless whisper escaped her lips as she sat up on her knees took the strap on dildo off and passed it to Daness.

Placing her hands flat onto my chest, she got right on top of me and slowly eased her way down. I would've made her put a condom on me, but it didn't matter. I planned on enjoying her raw because after I nutted that was it for the both of them.

"Ssshhh daddy, I love how this dick feels." She tossed her head back as Daness sat up and licked on Lee's nipples. That encouraged Lee to pop and tighten her pussy all over my dick which had me clenching my ass cheeks tight. She got into a squatting position and danced all over my dick.

Gliding my fingers down her back, I planted my hand firmly on her ass and squeezed, holding her up from the bottom, I moved her up and down faster as both of their moans intertwined with one another. Ten minutes later, I could feel my balls tightening, my dick started to twitch as Daness started to lick on Lee's swollen clit.

When Lee started to cum, I didn't hold back shooting my nut all inside of her. Smoothly pulling my gun from underneath me, I shot Lee right in the head just as she started to kiss Daness. Daness didn't have enough time to react because when she looked over at me, I put a bullet right between her eyes.

"Fuck off of me freak bitches. Should've never tried to

threaten me for more money." I wiped the sweat off of my forehead and maneuvered my way from around them. Picking up my cellphone I sent a text to my nigga Drew, letting him know that it was time for him to show up with his cleaning crew to get Daness and Lee out of my bedroom.

I dialed Princess' number and as usual, the bitch didn't pick up. I didn't know what it was that kept me loving on her fat trifling ass, but I couldn't let her go. I taught Princess every single thing she knew. She was part of my collection, my possession. No matter how far she tried to stray away from me, she knew that she would always be my bitch. The only bitch that could even say they've gotten close enough to a niggas heart.

I stepped into the shower to clean myself and get my mind right for today. A big smile crossed my face because for one I knew that I had that bitch ass nigga Midas in his feelings over his momma. I didn't give a fuck about Ms. Wellington, I didn't give a damn about anybody's momma or sparing feelings when I lost my momma.

Losing my momma was hard as fuck, but I got over that shit because I didn't want it to keep me down in the dumps and stuck inside of my feelings. I had missions to complete and the only thing that I was after was the almighty dollar. I didn't like to limit myself when it came to buying nice things.

Apart of being that nigga was having the bread to match my persona. I had money but the amount that I had didn't classify me to be a hood rich nigga.

"Histori?" I wiped my hand down the shower glass door to stare at Ariana. Ariana made my stomach churn; I was so close to giving her my size twelve foot to kiss.

"What?" I continued to scrub underneath my balls and dick to get any traces of Lee and Daness off of me.

"There's men that came in."

"And?" I looked back up at her through the shower glass and dared her to say some dumb shit. I was on edge and with the way I was feeling right now, I was ready to kill her stupid ass too.

"I never saw dead bodies before, I- umm... I don't want to go to jail, Histori." Her voice cracked as I chuckled in disbelief.

"Ariana, get the fuck up out of here and stay out of my business. I only allowed you to come to Vegas to see if you could hang with the high paid hoes. You too busy getting high and tooting that shit up your nose ain't gone get you to the big leagues, baby. I'm sending you back home in the morning. You wasting my time and money." I turned my back and rinsed my body off.

"Please Histori! I haven't gotten high in days now. I'm sorry, I just got a little nervous seeing those girls dead. Are you going to kill the older lady that's locked in the guest room?" I bowed my head under the shower head, letting the water run down my face and head. Shutting the water off, I stepped out of the shower dripping water everywhere.

I now had tunnel vision, my anger was probably misplaced since Ariana really seemed worried and concerned. It was something about her though that just annoyed the fuck out of me. Wrapping both hands around her neck, I let all of my anger take over as she clawed at my arms and hands.

Her eyes popped out of its sockets as she fought hard to breathe. Getting tired of squeezing her neck, I twisted her around and snapped her fucking neck, and released her limp body from my hands.

"Bitch just asking too many muh'fuckin questions." I snatched the towel from the rack and placed it around my waist. Opening up the bathroom door my room was already looking back to its regular state. I made eye contact with one of Drew's men and stopped him from walking out of the room.

"Tell Drew that there is an extra body in my bathroom. He can add her to my tab." I didn't wait for a response; I went right to my dresser to get out a pair of boxers and an undershirt. Dropping my towel, I quickly put on my undergarments and then pulled out a pair of sweats.

I looked in the mirror and offered myself a strained smile. I needed to trust the process of all of this shit and not let it stress me out. When it was all said and done, niggas would know that my reputation preceded itself and that I was not the nigga to be fucked with. I wasn't some ordinary nigga, and I was tired of niggas treating me like I was one.

This was considered reckless on my behalf, not having a concrete plan in motion. I just knew that by me having this nigga's mom I'd have the start of my plan to get more fuckin' money. Leaving out of my bedroom, I walked down the hallway ignoring the sound of my hoes calling me daddy.

I really wanted to tell these hoes to beat it and go make some money. They needed me for that, and I hadn't had the time to go through my contact list to set them up with dates. I had about five hoes that needed their hair and nails done. Before I could hit the steps that led to the guest room that I had Ms. Wellington in, a loud banging noise sounded throughout the entire house.

I crinkled my brows and turned to go see who was at my door late in the evening. As soon as I opened the door, I just shook my head and stepped to the side. The biggest mistake that I had made was fucking Princess' mom. Bitch was in love with me ever since I was seventeen.

"Patrice, what the fuck you doing in Vegas man?!" I pinched my brows together frustrated as hell now. She didn't

6

answer me, she eyed two of my hoes that were sitting on the couch with her lip snarled up like she was disgusted.

"I need to talk with you in private." I shook my head and licked my lips. I eyed her fine old ass like she'd be my next meal. Patrice was considered old, but she was sexy as fuck. That's why I wanted Princess, from looking at her momma who was in her late fifties, I imagined Princess when she got older.

Old women were freaks, they got right to the point, and they knew exactly what they wanted in the bedroom. Patrice was thick with a perfect Coke bottle shape to her.

"Princess never ask me to excuse my hoes. The fuck you think this is P? You better ask them to scoot over and wait for when I have the time. You still didn't answer my question. What the fuck is you doing all the way out here?" My jaws clenched. It had been a minute since the last time I put my foot up a bitch ass. I was tempted to make an example out of her old ass, coming up in here demanding some shit that she didn't have the rights to.

She looked down at her short French tip nails then back up at me with hopeful eyes.

"Well, you told me that you would be in Vegas. Since my husband is gone for a while, I figured I'd surprise you, this is our little getaway spot. I just didn't think that you would have company." Her eyes glossed up like they always did when she didn't get her way then an idea popped up in my head.

"How many free days you got from that nigga?" She perked up at that.

"About five days." Her smile reached her eyes.

"Fasho, well, since you old and all, I got an old bitch in the guest room that I need your help with. Go cook up something, it's food in the refrigerator. When you done, I'll explain to you more about the situation and how yo money hungry

7

ass can benefit from it since your daughter ain't here to assist me." She nodded her head slowly and then turned on her heels to walk away. Patrice was like thorns in a nigga side. If I killed her, it would be a relief too. She constantly had her hand out for money, and she even threatened a nigga a couple of times with telling Princess. The thought of killing her came to my mind a couple of times but I didn't want to violate Kane like that. He already hated the fact that I was fucking his momma and sister.

Plus, I liked the good ass head Patrice gave, her pussy still worked like she was in her prime, and she knew how to make that muthafucka talk.

Finally making my way to the basement, I cracked the door open and eyed Ms. Wellington down. Her eye was swollen shut but her pecan skin tone glowed. Her hair was all over her head, she looked like she was in high distress as she clutched her chest and looked up at me like she was seeing the devil.

"I really ain't want to do you like this. You're so sweet and don't deserve it but shit, you know how this type of thing goes. I don't want to kill you, but I might have to if Midas don't kick out what I'm asking for." I made it to the side of the bed where she was sitting. Opening the nightstand, I pulled out a long sharp blade to cut her wrist free, I stopped when she started to speak.

"I've lived my life, Histori. I lived a good ass gentle life at that. The only reason I look at you with fear in my eyes is because I can feel a demon in you. You as a man don't scare me, death don't scare me either. I'm sure whatever amount of money you want, my son will provide. If you're trying to hurt him deeply then go ahead and kill me. Just know that it takes a minute to pray and a second to die." She smirked as my stomach dropped from her boldness. She gave me a poker face and turned her head away from me, breathing a loud breath out causing her hair to move a little from in front of her lips.

"When you take money, it runs out fast, when you work hard for it, it sticks around longer. You're only making things worse for yourself. Either free my hands and let me get comfortable until my death. Or let me stay uncomfortable, with tied wrist. I honestly don't give a fuck. I see why my son told me to never accept a call from you. I don't have shit else to say, Histori." She turned her head and looked off into space.

My expression slid into a frown as my brows creased.

"You always thought that you were the head bitch in charge of something when really, you weren't running shit but that pussy. My father wanted me in on everything! That's why Midas brought me to the table, he fucked up by trying to act like he created all of what he's running." Now there was a deep-set frown covering her face.

"My son gave you a chance and you let greed take over you. He was meant to lead, and he added onto the foundation that he is sitting on. My husband wanted to make sure you were taken care of. He wanted Midas to guide you and help you become more but you wanted to go against that and not follow the lead!"

"Y'all hated me! My mom looked better than you and my father… your husband loved my mom just as much as he loved you!" I smirked as I sat down on the bed to taunt her.

"That's good for your father and mother. I often wondered why he cut her off… He was sick when I left him, he begged for his family back. I told him to make sure that he was a fair and good father to you, and he did that. After a year of him begging and us being separated, he came right back to me. I accepted you; I didn't remain bitter because you were involved, you came to my house. I fed you, bathed you, and made sure you got the same love as Midas. When it came time to take you back home, I did that as well. I never hated you Histori because if I did, I would have never accepted your calls or told my son that he needed to be there to support you for the passing of your mother." She chuckled and dropped her head. She moved her arms a little uncomfortably while trying to blink back tears.

"Insulting me won't work, I'm hurting because your father really wouldn't want this, and this is more of the reason why I don't want either you or Midas tied up in any illegal activities anymore, but I know I can't stop it. I'm also hurting because when it's all said and done... I can no longer stand in the way of my son trying to take your head off. Listen to me Histori and listen closely... we are now considered enemies; I will always stand with my son right or wrong. In this case, he has every right to protect his mother. Even if you were to set me free, it wouldn't change shit. Your days are numbered, there is no turning back from this. I just pray my son offers you some kind of mercy, this is the type of situation that leads to slow brutal torture. Go ask yourself if you're really prepared for that."

"I'm prepared for it all. To kill you and your son and become what I always was supposed to be. I'm just clearing my path, you keep talking and getting at me the way that you are, I'll torture you just how you keep claiming your son will torture me when he catches me."

I left her ass sitting in the same position, changing my mind about letting her wrist go free. I needed to smoke and get some head from Patrice to clear my mind and ease my worries. Deep down, I knew that I was no match for Midas. The nigga had connections that were way above what I was equipped with. I only had him by the balls, Maybe I should have tried to get back cool with Midas but now it was too late for that. I could get this money now, but I needed him and his entire organization dead to enjoy the money. In order for me to step in his shoes, Midas had to die along with anyone connected to him.

That was a hard task, and by the time I demanded more money from him, I needed a better plan in motion. I couldn't sleep at night thinking of what Ms. Wellington spoke about. Midas catches me and tortures me until he kills me. One thing I was afraid of was dying because I wanted to live. Shit was fucking with me heavily.

NAYVIUS

"*W*atch what you say around this nigga Midas. Real shit Shooter, I ain't gon' lie to you. Niggas been looking at you funny and shit my nigga. That shit with Darius had to happen and you know it. I ain't even saying that it didn't affect me and Midas 'cause it fucked with me but the nigga violated. This is momma, I say momma like she mine because when my momma left, she stepped in and gave a nigga the same love and affection that my momma gave me. Midas is in another element right now. You know I'm the nigga that's always out of line and acting off impulse. Midas is in that type of zone. You my nigga and I don't want shit else going left." I lifted the bottle of Remy and took two big gulps. I could feel myself staggering a little as the night wind blew across my face making me feel at ease since my stomach was hot as fuck and growing queasy.

I always thought I could control my liquor, but once I started it was hard for me to stop. The liquor always gave me that feeling of relaxation. Whenever I was stressed, it eased that and all the tension I was feeling. It placed me in a different time zone, I'd momentarily forget about whatever was stressing me. It took my pain away and made all the trauma that I had going through my head freeze. It was hard staying sober because being sober made me face all my problems. Having to deal with too many raw emotions had me acting off emotion and like Midas would always say, that working off emotion alone could get a nigga caught up.

Shooter and I stood at the front door of Ms. Wellington's house. Midas has been staying here for the past week trying to get the proper lead on his mom. Shit was fucking us all up because Ms. Wellington was a sweet ass lady. She didn't deserve this shit. It was fucking with Midas hard because, for the first time, he felt like he failed to protect her.

I told Shooter what was all going on because no matter the differences we had we were all boys.

"Nigga you ain't gotta school me when it comes to that nigga. You know I say how the fuck I feel and if I disagree with the way a nigga moved, I'm gone express that too." Shooter puffed his chest out and I shook my head.

"I'm upset with the nigga but I'm still down for niggas. Ms. Wellington has always been good to me. That nigga Histori should've been put in the dirt. Look what all this nigga been up to." I hated to admit it, but Shooter was right. Midas was reluctant to kill his brother and now the damage was done.

Shooter balled up his fist to knock on the front door but Midas already was opening up the front door with red-rimmed eyes like he was high out of his mind. He eyed Shooter for a long time, and I prayed that this nigga didn't bust a nutty. Shooter pulled Midas into a manly embrace and Midas patted Shooter back hard. Shooter patted Midas's back as they just stood like that for seconds which felt like minutes.

"You were right, my nigga, I should've killed that nigga. I

still stand on business though. You switched up on me, I never thought you would ever turn your back on me. I wouldn't switch shit if we went back in time. Darius had to die; we know the rules to this. I can be man enough to say that you were right on behalf of Histori, that nigga belongs in the dirt, and I spared him when he didn't try to spare me. Sometimes water can be thicker than blood. Now we on some Cain and Abel type shit." Midas pulled back from the hug, pinching the bridge of his nose. I hated seeing this nigga like how he was at the moment. Seeing your homie always being strong, that when you finally see him weak it seems foreign. My boy was hurting and all I wanted was for things to get back on track. Something in the pits of my stomach was telling me that things would change. I had the same sick feeling that I had when my parents were murdered.

"We gon' get that nigga. I already got Sonya on the way with a resume on all that nigga hoes. She gon' research every last one of them to see if they got any property in their names so we can track him down. You know dumb ass niggas like him can't get shit in their name, so they put shit in their bitches or momma's name." We all nodded our heads in agreement.

Shooter was always smart as fuck and any time a problem arose, he played chess and tried to get ahead of whatever the problem was. We walked into the house, I shut and locked the door behind me, and frowned my face up immediately. Inhaling sharply, I exhaled and turned to look over at Midas.

"Nigga you done lost yo fuckin' mind." I looked around the front room. Midas had his momma's house smelling like weed and liquor. That was unlike him because he never smoked inside of his own house like that unless he felt the need to and even then, he aired that shit out. He never wanted the weed smell around his mom out of respect.

Midas had about twenty guns lying around like he was preparing for war.

"Where is my Bible?" I asked no one in particular.

"For what nigga?" Shooter asked as Midas raised his brows.

"I don't know man... feels like it's too much sin around me up in Momma Wellington's house. When we bring her back here, I don't want no parts from the ass whooping she gon' give you." I hiccupped and tasted nothing but alcohol. I stumbled toward the couch moving the AR-15 that was in my way and sat down.

"Nigga always joking. Remind me to have the driver take you home. I keep telling you to stop driving drunk and partially blind." Midas took a seat in his mom's favorite loveseat.

"Nigga always tryna big brother me, I'm good nigga. I got Jaiden waiting for me at the crib. I ain't even drunk, just tipsy as hell." I held the bottle up and shook my head at myself. Half of the bottle was gone. I couldn't go around Jaiden like this, so I sat the bottle down and went in my pocket to pull out some weed to smoke. The weed would mellow me out.

"He wants ten million. The amount is crazy, but I got it already. He called earlier demanding the shit by Friday. That's three days, three days with my momma getting treated fucked up by this nigga." Midas jaws clenched tight.

"I told him to let me hear her voice, he let me hear her, but she was crying. She couldn't even talk." Midas' voice broke causing me and Shooter to look up at him. He was forcing back his emotions. Pinching the bridge of his nose again he looked off away from us as I sparked the blunt, feeling guilty about even sparking a blunt up in his mom's house.

"Alright three days it is then, but when Sonya gets here in a minute, we lessen those three days into one. I know you hurting. Having a nigga by the balls hurts especially when you used to calling the shots and now it's like you got to tread carefully for the sake of mom dukes. That nigga gon' pay, on my kids he will pay." A dark look crossed Shooter's face and I could feel all of our anger for the situation bouncing off of each other.

My phone ringing took my attention away from the conversation we were having. I saw that it was Jaiden Face-time calling me, so I stood up and walked down the long hallway that led to the open kitchen area. Midas lived in a smaller home, but Ms. Wellington's house was like a mini castle down to the expensive decorations.

I answered the call and Jaiden's face was frowned up like she was pissed with me. I gave her a lazy smirk then bit into my bottom lip. I never got enough of seeing her pretty ass face. Her ocean blue eyes twinkled every time she stared at me. When she wasn't around, I'd close my eyes and still could see her pretty round chubby face.

"Damn, you over there looking sexy as fuck. I bet you smell sweet too huh?" She smacked her lips and rolled her eyes.

"Nayvius, it is hard for a woman with two kids to get a babysitter. I did not drive all the way to this uppity ass neigh-borhood on a school night to have a movie night with you for you not to be here. I've been here for over an hour!" Her voice elevated and my dick grew hard immediately. This was a new side of Jaiden; I liked it because she wasn't afraid to speak her mind.

She just didn't understand the personal shit that I was facing when it came to Midas' momma missing. Shit was real right now, I lost track of time.

"I know baby, I'm gon' make it up to you. I'm bout to leave here in like twenty minutes." I guessed wrong.

"Get comfortable, I told you that you didn't even need a sitter. You could've brought the kids. I got enough room for them too."

"I think not Nay. If we are just dating then the kids will not be introduced to you until we become serious. Which looks like a long road ahead of us. I won't play with my kids' feelings just because we both are digging each other."

"I respect that. I won't even rush you, but you know that I'm feeling yo pretty ass. I'm willing to put the work in." Jaiden just brought on a different side of me. Half the time, I couldn't even recognize myself when talking to her. It's like I became somebody else without even trying.

"So far, you're not doing so good putting in the work. This supposed to be a date night for us. I didn't expect you this late, and I don't feel comfortable in your house without you here. You know what? I think I'm going to just go. I understand your type of line of work better than you think I do. Things come up; I totally get it. Maybe we will just try for a different time." I could see her moving around my living room as the pit of my stomach fell.

I wanted to come home to Jaiden tonight, she didn't even know how much peace she brought to my chaotic lifestyle.

"Jai... Don't leave baby. I got some heavy shit going on, on my end but I promise you that a nigga bout to leave in a minute."

"It's not a big deal, Nay. I'll just see you tomorrow. My brother wants to take the girls shopping tomorrow and Rodrik is supposed to keep them at his mom's house tomorrow night." She licked her lips; I watched her closely and noticed her purse on her shoulder. I started to pace the kitchen while pulling at my chin hairs.

17

"Jaiden, it is a big deal to me, mommas. A real big deal. I want to see… I need to see you, on some real shit. Just chill out for me and I promise, I'll make the shit worth it. Damn, you want me to start begging already." I chuckled nervously.

"You do look sexy right now begging Nayvius. Okay, you got an hour… that's even too long but I'll give you that since you say you got some heavy shit going on." She rolled her eyes, and I promised her that I'd be there before the hour was up and hung up. I turned to walk out of the kitchen and Midas stood at the entrance of the kitchen with a blank expression plastered on his face.

"Sonya here?" I broke the silence. Midas chuckled, and then his chuckle turned into a full-blown laugh from the gut.

"I can always count on you, Goof."

"For what?"

"To make a nigga laugh when I really feel like bitching up and crying. Man, you already in love with that girl." Midas walked towards the refrigerator, opened it, and pulled out three beers.

"I'm just feeling her, that's it." I waved him off.

"Nigga feeling her? You just excused yourself from our conversation to answer her call. That's a good look for you, real shit. Just don't fuck it up." He patted my shoulder, and I just nodded my head because he had me right there. I ain't never excused myself for when a female called. I didn't even do that shit for my ex-Vanessa and I really loved her weird ass.

"Sonya in there on her laptop we gon' be up for a while writing down information. So far, she pulled up one of his hoes that got property in Vegas. It's the furthest property connected to him so be ready early am. We going to Vegas."

"Fasho, I'll be through early am then." We slapped hands and then embraced each other into a brotherly hug. I said my goodbyes to Shooter and Sonya and did a hundred all the way home to make it to Jaiden's demanding ass.

* * *

I RUBBED Jaiden's slightly swollen feet then slipped my fingers between her toes. Holding the blunt between my lips the smoke kept blowing in my eyes causing my shit to water. I passed Jaiden the blunt and she raised her eyebrows and shook her head no.

I was surprised when I got home and smelled food throughout my entire house. That was some shit that I wasn't used to but could get real used to fast. Jaiden claimed that she was bored waiting on me, so she went into my kitchen and saw that I had her favorite meat inside my refrigerator. Lamb chops, she whipped them up with gravy served over home-made mashed potatoes with a salad on the side.

"I don't smoke," I smirked at her just admiring her beauty. The feel of the bottom of her feet was soft and silky. I kept massaging with my free hand as I held the blunt out for her to take it from my hand.

"You don't gotta smoke baby, just hold daddy blunt while I make you feel good." She looked at the blunt like it was foreign, and after a couple of seconds passed, she finally hit it, quickly blowing the smoke out without inhaling it.

"Man, you wasting my shit. You 'pose to inhale it and hold it for a couple seconds." She giggled and puckered her lips to hit it a second time. She inhaled and started to choke hard with her face frowned up, holding her chest. Jaiden was dramatic as fuck, but I liked that shit. She got beside herself hitting the blunt two more times without choking.

I eased my hands up her calves until I reached her thick thighs. I loved her fuckin' thighs, they were so damn thick

19

and sexy that I couldn't help touching them whenever they were exposed. I watched her closely; her eyes were low as fuck. My hands went to her inner thighs, and she opened her legs wide for me.

"You feeling freaky, Jaiden?" She nodded her head up and down then hit the blunt again.

"You want me to eat this pussy while my chains slide up and down yo ass cheeks?" I eyed her fat pussy, and my mouth watered. I dove right in not giving her a chance to answer my question.

"Mmm Nay." She moaned as I used both my hands to keep her legs parted like the sea. Dipping my tongue in and out of her hot tunnel, I dragged it to her clit and flattened it applying constant pressure. My dick twitched, the taste of her had pre cum oozing from the head of my dick.

Jaiden's pussy was aqua fresh when the pussy tasted this clean it made a nigga freakier. Her body trembled, my tongue left her clit alone and went back to her sticky tunnel. I tried to make my tongue go even deeper, I wanted my tongue to find and hit her G spot while I massaged her clit with the tip of my nose.

I inhaled the pussy and then drunk down her juices like I needed it to survive. She coughed a little and I knew she had hit the blunt again making her even higher. Spreading her ass cheeks, I paused for a couple of seconds and smiled.

"Damn I'm really bout to be on some freaky shit." I shook my head a little, mumbling to myself.

"Huh?" She sat up on her elbows a little.

"Nothing baby, lay back and neck that blunt." I rubbed my hand over her clit then spread her ass cheeks again. I ain't never ate a female's ass before and didn't know what the fuck to expect. I loved how big Jaiden's booty was, so I had to have a taste of this shit too.

I eyed her asshole and went in using my tongue flickering it and teasing her asshole, Jaiden damn near tried to climb the headboard.

"Ohhh wait, Nayvius! What you doing?" I chuckled lowly, taking her thighs, and locking them in my arms as I kissed each ass cheek then dove back in. She moaned till she was hoarse; I followed the line next to her asshole with my tongue licking until my tongue was back inside of her contracting pussy. Her clit was swollen so I gave it some more attention, lapping her like a dog.

Jaiden started to cum, and my dick started to jerk by itself. Fuck she was making me nut on myself. Jaiden had me on some sprung ass nigga shit. Our connection was out of this world.

I was lost all inside of tasting her sweet essence. She erupted all over my tongue and I damn near licked her dry. Right now, I wasn't thinking clearly. All I saw was Jaiden, all I wanted was Jaiden. God didn't give up on my dark ass heart. I think he created her just for me and sent her my way when he knew I'd need her the most.

"I think... nah... I know that I..." *Love you,* I thought to myself. I loved her, and I was falling in love with her. I didn't even know it until now. Looking into her low pretty eyes.

"What were you bout to say?" She smiled and giggled a little. Her legs were shaking under me like she was still riding the wave of coming all over my tongue. My face felt cold from her juices drying up. Her scent was alluring, it had me growing back hard. I grabbed my dick and stroked myself until I was fully standing to attention.

"Jaiden, I'm about to fuck the shit out of you mommas like real shit. If a nigga going to hard let me know. You say we just dating because it's all too soon and I'm gon' respect that shit for now. Just don't play around with that dating shit.

Understand that to a nigga like me... I view you as mine. I'm bout to write my name all over you in permanent dick ink. Can't no other nigga have you but me. Real fuckin' spill." I eyed her nipples then focused back on her eyes.

Her body glowed like she had a full body halo surrounding her. My room, the bed and everything surrounding us faded into the background. I felt myself getting sucked into only her, as I studied and outlined her luscious thick body sitting in front of me and pulled her close until her nipples pressed against my body.

I kissed her shoulders then her neck, letting my lips travel to her plump lips. I didn't even know how to kiss like that, but her tongue danced around with mine. Laying her down on her back my dick knocked up against her wet pussy. Her eyes widen as I took control of my dick, sliding it up and down between her wet folds.

Growling lowly anticipation getting the best of me, I entered her and sat still at just her opening; I bowed my head in surrender because she got me. She got me hooked and I knew at this moment that I better pace myself. I can't nut early inside of her. I'd be lying if I said that the pussy wasn't the best that I ever encountered.

It contracts tightly and molds around my dick like it was created for only me. The pussy is pulsating around my dick. It feels like her pussy is suctioning my dick in then out. A pussy with its own heartbeat is insane and might even sound farfetched but I swear I feel it right now. I shook my head and started slow stroking her. Jaiden looked me right in the eyes as she began to thrust herself into me, moving her hips in a rotating motion.

"Fuck, baby." I groaned and told her to slow the fuck down. My phone started to ring, and I hesitated at moving, as Jaiden kept fucking me back while rubbing my chest with her soft fingertips. I was losing my mind as the phone stopped ringing and started back up again.

"Fuck!" I frowned, never stopping my strokes. I reached over to grab my phone off the nightstand and I saw that it was Shooter.

"Yo." I slowed down my pace and tried to catch my breath.

"Midas ain't waiting, he on one. We bout to hit Princess' momma's house and run down on her brother Kane."

"Fuck he got to do with anything." I slowly pulled out of Jaiden, she gave me a perplexed look as I got off the bed with my dick aching to be back inside of her.

"Get here fast, nigga." Shooter hung up, as I tossed my phone on the bed and went right to my bathroom to clean Jaiden's juices off my dick. She wouldn't understand and she probably would be mad at me. I cared how she felt but I had to dip. This was how shit was for me, and for my niggas, I would ride till the end, it's all I knew.

MIDAS

earing all black matched my mood. I couldn't get any proper rest; it wasn't fair to my momma. She was somewhere being held against her will for a couple of M's while I was out free waiting to hear a meet-up location to get her in exchange for the money.

Nah shit wasn't about to go down this way. I wasn't a wait-for-instructions type of man. I wanted my mom safe asap. The more days and nights I went without sleep, the more delirious I got.

I watched Shooter and Goof watch me waiting to see what I was waiting and watching for. We had been sitting outside of Princess' momma's house for the past two hours, the lights were out. No cars were parked indicating that anyone was home until I saw a compact all red Kia pull up into the driveway.

"There he is," I mumbled to myself, adrenaline taking over and getting the best of me. It's been a long time since I even did some shit like this. I hadn't gotten my hands dirty for a couple of years now. This right here was some personal shit.

"What we doing?" Goof reached for the door handle, I placed my hand on his shoulder, shaking my head no.

"Look." I pointed lowly. I looked back at Shooter, and he already knew what timing I was on. I looked directly at Kane and could see him clearly. The woman he was with put her arms around his neck, kicking her right leg backwards in the air like she was in love and infatuated with him. Kane kept looking around, checking out the surroundings of his momma's house. It was obvious that he felt something in his gut but couldn't quite place it because he had his girl touching all over him. Fucking up his first mind and judgment.

"A nigga always knows when something ain't right. His best move right now would be to get his bitch back in the car and drive off. He looks around because he feels something that he should follow. Instead, he wants to believe that he's tripping and paranoid. He's too focused on getting his dick wet now, that's going to cost him." I opened the middle console pulling out my black leather gloves.

"Always go with your first mind, even when you don't want to." Saying nothing else, I opened my door and got out of the car. The cold night air hit my face, as I walked away from my car, leaving the door wide open. It was so quiet that I didn't have to even raise my voice to get Kane's attention.

Crossing the street, I pulled my gun and lowered it to my side.

"Kane." He froze and I was disappointed in him. He didn't go to reach for a weapon or attempt to cover himself.

"I'm a nigga on edge right now Kane." I kicked a couple of rocks in front of me and eyed Kane seriously.

"I guess it's what the younger generation calls it… down bad." Shrugging nonchalantly, I stood at the bottom of the driveway. I didn't have to look behind me to feel Shooter and

Goof right behind me who were now standing on each side of me.

Goof chuckled lowly and clicked his teeth. He approached Kane and his woman, she now stood holding on to Kane for dear life. The closer Goof got the harder the woman shook.

"If you scream, you're going to cause problems." Goof grabbed her wrist, prying her away from Kane. He stood stuck in place, not saying a word like he was trying to process what was all going down in front of him. The sound of water sprinkling on the ground sounded off and it was his girl pissing herself.

"You can leave, baby girl. Your man will be fine. He just has to comply with me and then maybe tomorrow you two can pick up where you left off here, yea?" She slowly nodded her head and wiped at her tears. Kane didn't say shit still, the look on his face would've been comical if he owed me some money. Right now, he owed me direct answers.

As his girl got in the car. Goof searched him and came up empty-handed. I shook my head at that.

"It takes a minute to pray, and a second to die. It's clear you're green as fuck Kane. As a man living in L.A., you should never be out here naked, without a gun." His girl pulled off, and I didn't bother taking any steps towards him.

"Let's go inside so we can talk."

"Mannnn…" Kane drawled, finally finding his voice.

"Inside Kane." I moved my gun, pointing towards his front door with it. In defeat, his shoulders dropped as he picked up his feet. Once he got his front door open, Shooter and Goof flipped the sofas in the living room checking for weapons. I closed the front door and leaned up against the door with my head tilted backwards a little.

"I'm a man of patience and understanding. But like I said outside, I'm down bad. My mother was taken against her will and for that, people are going to fucking die. Now I don't want you to act as if you don't know who the fuck, I am Kane. You know who I am. You know what all I'm capable of. Don't give me a I don't know what's going on kind of speech because you do. I can very well be in the mood to make you feel how I feel. Like your sister Princess, your father and mother can be missing but not at a fee. You won't even have the resources or the reach to get back at me for them. So, tell me what the fuck I want to hear so we can go get my muthafuckin' momma. I'm losing my cool and once it's gone, I'm going to fuckin' snap." I snapped my fingers together and Kane jumped.

"I didn't do-"

Pow! I purposely aimed and shot his foot. He immediately collapsed and started to sob out loud. My blood began to boil, cracking my neck from side to side usually calmed me down, but right now the gesture wasn't working.

"Tell me what the fuck I want to hear nigga!" My voice bounced off the walls, I stood up straight and marched towards him with tunnel vision. Goof and Shooter stepped out of my way as I neared him.

"You ain't hear what the fuck I just said to you? Ya momma, daddy, and sister can be gone on an account of you fuckin' around with me right now!" My jaws clenched; my body was locked up with so much rage that I could feel my blood boiling. Hearing his whimpering and crying out for help made me think of my mom. Was she crying and whimpering too? Asking for help, wondering where the fuck I was to protect her? I stepped on the foot that I had shot Kane in and used all of my weight to stand on it.

Feeling more rage because he hadn't said shit except for

crying out for God's deliverance. I started kicking him all over his pathetic ass body until I felt myself growing tired.

"My mom is fucking Histori! She went to be with him in Vegas! It's where they always meet up at, so my dad won't know. I don't know shit about yo momma man I swear on my life I don't know. Histori and I don't talk like that. He be thinking I'm dumb! I know what he does with my momma. My sister gets on my nerves but it's wrong what they doing to Princess because she fucking loves him man!" He cried out in pain. Drool seeped out of his mouth as he grabbed at his wounded foot.

"I swear to you, I ain't with that street shit. I don't know nothing man, I been stop fucking with that nigga. You gotta believe me." He sniffled but the snot was running out from his nose mixed with blood. Goof started to laugh hard, clutching his stomach.

"This grown ass nigga really laying there crying like a lil bitch? Nigga been farting and shit, got the whole room smelling like egg. Shut the fuck up and man up nigga." Goof's silly smirk faded away from his face, he now had that crazy look in his eyes as he clutched his gun tighter. Goof was ready to kill, he was always more trigger happy than Shooter. Shooter had the best aim out of all of us, which was how he got his name.

"Get something to wrap his foot with. He's coming with us to Vegas." I walked out the front door anxious to take a five-hour drive to go get my momma. Princess crossed my mind in the process. She was really dealt a bad hand, with the nigga she decided to fall in love with and her own family.

I hadn't discussed her any further with Diamond because he was more concerned with me finding my mom. It told me everything that I needed to know about my son, and I understood now why he had a street name, such as Logic. The lil nigga was smart as fuck he was young but wise. It also told me that I still had time to teach him a few things and possibly one day turn everything over to him.

Did I want Princess with my boy? Hell nah, but if he chose to still fuck with her after the bit of information that I gave him on her, that was totally up to him. I wouldn't feel any type of way, I just really wouldn't trust her. I was killing Histori, there was no other way around that. If anyone stepped in my way or tried to get back at me for his bitch ass, then they could get fed with lead as well.

I eyed the front Shooter and Goof walking behind Kane. With each step Kane took his face winced out in pain as he was walking on his injured foot. Starting up the car my pulse slammed in my neck. I couldn't believe that this nigga Histori really had the audacity to take my momma.

* * *

THE ENTIRE RIDE WAS QUIET, I drowned the sound of Kane whimpering and crying the entire way and smoked blunt after blunt to keep myself from losing my cool.

"Midas you need a bigger truck, I mean we all over six feet, and this shit is cramped up like a bitch." Goof complained while trying to stretch his long legs in the front seat.

"Nigga you need to be worried about hygiene. Running out the house smelling like budussy and shit." Shooter chuckled as I turned down a block that looked to be a cul-de-sac. The block was quiet, the sun started to rise, it was still cloudy and dark. Wintertime in California always had the weather bipolar.

"You tryna say my girl pussy and ass stank nigga? The fuck is budussy?" Goof opened my glove compartment and pulled out two sets of leather gloves, tossing a setback to Shooter, he turned a little to look over at him.

"It means just what you said, ass and pussy. I smelled a whiff of it earlier when you was running your mouth."

"Nigga my girl don't stank. Her ass and pussy taste good as fuck, watch it, Shooter." Goof eyed him seriously just as Shooter started to laugh lowly.

"Damn nigga, we got you hitting the blunt and you really out here eating ass. That's cold as fuck, so I guess it's like we all ate her ass and pussy since we been having you in rotation with the weed."

"Cut that shit, let's suit up." Without breaking eye contact, I pointed to the house with the address that I had memorized by heart.

"How we moving in?" Shooter asked, my eyebrows raised because I hadn't even thought of that.

"Go in, search. Make yourselves invisible." I ordered. We all knew how to do that without a problem.

"I'll be in… soon." I eyed the two-story home as if I already had a layout of it.

"Quick question, you want the nigga alive right?" Goof held the door handle.

"Correct." I nodded my head.

"Okay, so…when we get moms we taking him with us… How we all 'pose to fit in this car?" I looked at Shooter through the mirror and could tell he was holding back his laugh.

"I do have a trunk nigga, Kane and Histori besties, they will hold hands lying down next to each other." I smirked as Goof couldn't hold his laugh to save his life. I shook my head at Goof and watched both of them get out of the car and leave out.

"My brother…" I turned and looked at Kane who looked even more scared now.

"He's entitled and feels like what's mine should be his. He doesn't understand that we are nothing alike. I never expected to make the amount of money that I now make. Have a certain status as well as connections. People see me and view me as something I don't even view myself as. My father always told me that I had the Midas Touch when it came to anything. Sometimes I don't find that to be so true. I wanted to keep my brother alive because my father loved him. He wanted us to be close, and I tried that shit and it backfired. Histori is better off dead. A man of greed will cross his own flesh and blood a million times until he feels as if he succeeded. I'm giving you free game right now. Listen closely, Greed makes people focus only on their personal fulfillment and satisfaction, ignoring values, everything becomes excessive to them. It makes you have anger and jealousy and can place you in an unhealthy competition. How can someone like that take over something that took years to fucking build. If I had greed, I wouldn't be here to get my mother. If it was the other way around, Histori would have said his mother lived a long life and that it was time for her to go. My lesson is greed fucks a lot of people up in life. In my line of business, it gets you killed. Honest to God truth, I never wanted to do what I am about to do now, but Histori took it there and now I will end it here."

I pulled my black ski mask from my middle console and placed it over my face. Pulling my hood over my head, I reached for the door handle.

"You can run or try your best to make it back to L.A. Help your sister out, get her on the right track. Warn her, if she fucks with my son Logic then she will be just like this nigga Histori. He already fucked her up enough, including your momma. Who I will try my best to spare." I got out of the car and headed towards the front. The closer I got the more I was able to see.

Every house on this block looked clean and nice, perfect lawns with flower beds, except this house. I eyed a tampon laying in the middle of the lawn with disgust. The grass was dry as hell and trash was thrown around like nobody ever took the time to clean the place.

Before I could reach the first step, Goof opened the front door with a solemn expression on his face.

"We gotta move fast my nigga." I felt the stress building in my chest, in the pits of my stomach fear collided with anxiety.

"We aired this muthafucka out, no lie... we found your mom upstairs with a gunshot wound in her right cheek. She got a pulse but it's fading." My knees buckled. I didn't hit the floor because Goof held me up, but he might as well had snatched my heart right out of my chest and stepped on it.

"What you saying, Nayvius?" I eyed him like he was telling a lie to me for the first time.

"We gotta get a move on it man. We got Histori, Shooter tied him up, they're in the garage in one of his cars. He's going to take him to the warehouse. Right now, Midas... we gotta get your mom to a hospital, asap my nigga. You gotta hold shit together and not fold right now. We gotta get a move on things ASAP." I nodded my head and swallowed down hard, blinking back the tears that my eyelids held hostage. Goof slowly stepped to the side and my eyes instantly fell on my mom's limp body. It felt like I was stuck in mud, I couldn't pick my legs up for the life of me.

"I can't believe I let him do this to you Ma." I dropped my head feeling defeated already. I was scared of the outcome of all of this. A violent storm was about to erupt, and

I couldn't see clearly through the fog. The muscles in my shoulders were tight as hell as the rest of my body cramped up with hate and anger.

Sparks of anger started to ignite me the closer I got to my mother. She looked dead but I wouldn't believe that even if God came down to take her to Heaven himself. I scooped her up in my arms and followed Goof out the front door with tunnel vision.

"Get on the line, I need her airlifted immediately." Was the last thing I said before I felt myself moving on autopilot getting inside of the backseat with my mom in my arms. Kane was gone and that was good for him, the way that I was feeling right now, I'd probably kill him just because of his ties to Histori. I could kill anyone right now to appease the way that I was feeling.

I cradled my mom in my arms and sat still.

"Momma, you know I can't take this. I know you strong, but I need you even stronger momma. I can't take you..." I struggled with breathing, I felt nauseous as I tried to swallow down spit, but my mouth was dry as hell. The faster Goof drove the dizzier I got. My heart started to beat rapidly as I felt an immense amount of pressure in my chest. Everything started to fade, and it suddenly felt like I was dying as everything went dark and my thoughts and panic stopped suddenly.

JAIDEN

I hated climbing steps, and it seemed like my mom lived up four flights of steps. I made it to her front door and stopped before putting my key in to listen in on all the commotion.

"Why the hell do you keep bringing this up Aubry? Jaiden is doing fine, and she is my child to worry about!" I frowned at the mention of Aubry being here. I only came here today because my mother wanted to make dinner and Rodrik was meeting me here to drop the kids off.

"She's my daughter, I want her to know that. I have grandkids that I would love to get to know. I can't keep going in life with this on my chest and in my heart. She looks just like me and her grandmother. She has my mother's eyes and my dimples; she is a miracle and I want to be a part of her life. I will no longer stand down Cherry. I let you run me off once, but I want her to at least know. She can hate me for it, but I just need her to know."

Everything went still and quiet, I could hear the whir of car tires on pavement, as someone honked their horn. Police sirens sounded off at a great distance as my hands grew clammy. I stood in front of my mom's door wide eyed not wanting to believe what I was hearing.

This entire time my biological mother was my teacher.

"I won't be working at the college anymore after this semester, maybe that will give you time to tell her. I took a job back at the hospital and I'm now back on call which will make me back busy. I want to make more money to be there for Jaiden to help her out more with the kids. She catches the bus to school and work from what I understand."

"Why do you want to be involved so bad? She's a product of rape!" My mom stunned me with her tone of voice. She always talked so sweetly, never saying mean things, so to hear her talk this way had me wondering what her deal was.

"I'm not going to let you mistreat or use her once you start seeing the resemblance of your sick ass stepfather!"

"You're trying to hurt me; Cherry and it won't work. I just want my daughter to know who I am. She is grown now, I have my own money, how or why would I use her?"

"You threw her in the trash, Aubry. When I got Jaiden, she was a broken little girl with sad eyes and scared to talk. She went from home to home; it was me that raised and helped build the confidence that she has now. It was me that made her happy and gave her stability. I won't let you swoop in and take that from me." My mom's voice broke, my tears started to fall before I could stop them, I decided that I had heard enough.

With shaky hands, I inserted the key and opened the door. My mom and Aubry both looked over at me with shock and pain written all over their faces and I didn't know what to exactly say.

"I never thought you would hide something from me." I looked over at my mom and she offered me a shamed face, full of guilt.

"Jaiden... I didn't want to hurt you."

"Well, you did." I snorted, my sadness turning into anger. I eyed Cherry like she was a stranger, I couldn't pick up my feet to move but I had enough energy to take my phone out of my purse and text Rodrik to let him know to keep the girls a little longer and I would meet with him at his mother house to pick them up.

"Jai Jai, come and sit down, baby, I never meant to lie to you. I just wanted to protect you." I wanted to say that it was bullshit, but I knew deep down it wasn't. I understood that people make mistakes and bad decisions all the time. It's why I always gave people grace with certain situations. I had no doubt in my mind that Cherry loved me. She raised me just like any mother should. Her keeping my biological mother away from me wasn't right and it wasn't her right to make that decision.

"I don't want to sit down Ma. You hurt me bad, you hurt me because you sat up with me plenty of nights when I was a kid up until I became an adult. I begged you to find my real mom just so I can know her and see what she looks like and ask her why did she throw me away. What was wrong with me that she didn't want to keep me?" My heavy eyes misted over as I looked over at Aubry who was wiping her face.

"I was young, too young. I was disgusted with myself, and I didn't deserve you. I don't want to sit here and make excuses for myself because what I did was selfish but looking back at the young me, I didn't know what to do. My stepfather was the devil. He had no remorse, no care for anything that he did. I was ten years old when I became a woman, a grown woman..." her voice was as light as a feather as her face went through a series of emotions.

Looking up at me, Aubry gave me a haunted expression.

She rubbed up and down her arms, like she caught a chill then continued to speak.

"I still sometimes smell all of the blood from my mother, from him and the blood between my legs. I remember how the argument started and how my mom was finally able to see the true monster that he was. She found kid porn in his phone and told him that she wanted a divorce. She threatened to expose him and a lot of other things she said in the heat of the moment that made him snap. He killed her, when he killed her, he came right after me. He told me that he would rather die happy than sad, not living out his wildest fetishes. Back then I was so frail and small. He didn't hold back and till this day that feeling of him tearing away at my innocence still haunts me. When he was done, he got a gun and put the pistol right into his mouth and killed himself." She sobbed out loud and rocked back in forth, like she was in a zone of her own.

Aubry had an absent look in her eyes like she was locked in the past being tormented by it. She kept gasping, taking deep breaths like she was struggling to breathe. For the first time since I walked inside of my mom's house, I took steps towards Aubry, gravitating to her pain, wanting to console and be there for her. I got down on my knees in front of her and reached for her gently.

Her sob turned into weeping, her stream of tears fell onto me, and I could no longer hold my own set of tears back.

"I don't want you to feel sorry for me baby. It's something that happened, but I have got to get it off my chest. I been in therapy and my late husband that passed away never got to see this raw side of me because I held back. He was so patient with me and understanding. I went on google and showed him the news clipping and let him do his own research. I told him I never wanted to relive or speak about it to anyone. I don't want my burden to belong to anyone but God. I told my husband that I wouldn't allow myself to have any more kids until I made things right with you. It was a punishment to myself for what I did to you Jaiden and I'm so sorry. I'm so damn sorry and if you never forgive me then I will completely understand. I was scared thinking you would look like him, I went from home to home, never knowing where I would land. I got abused mentally, physically, and emotionally. It's why I'm so aggressive and overprotective. I buried what my stepfather did to me and learned the way of the Lord. Once I was able to forgive him, I was ready to face you. That's when I started to beg Cherry to let me tell you. That was when my husband was still alive. Cherry was trying to protect you and she loved you as hers so please don't be upset with her. I felt like it was God placing me and Cherry at the same job together at the hospital. I was able to see you as you grew and then when me and her fell out it was like I was back feeling depressed. Then God placed us together again, when you walked through the door of my classroom."

She placed her hands on each side of my face and wiped at my tears.

"I love you Jaiden, and for the record, you look nothing like him. You got your blue eyes from my mom. She looked like an angel just like you. Only difference is she was chocolate, you took after my light caramel complexion and wavy thick hair." I smiled through my sadness.

"I love you too." My heart thumped hard as I threw my arms around her. We stayed hugged-up for minutes as we swayed with one another from side to side.

"I'm sorry Jaiden, I have no excuses anymore either for what I did. I feel horrible now, hearing Aubry's story. I want to take accountability for that and say that I'm so sorry Aubry. I should've been a better friend to you. I should have been there for you when your husband passed away. I can't have kids, so when I got Jaiden and Daymonte, I never wanted to lose them. I created a bond and didn't want to see that bond go away. Jaiden is such a loving person; I shouldn't have felt that way because I know that she has enough room to love us all."

"You right Ma, I do. I won't stop calling you mom because you were a good mother to me, and you always have been there loving any doubt right out of me. I hate that you felt that way as if I'd find my real mom and just forget about you. My mind can go back to before I came to you. I felt lost and not loved like I didn't belong anywhere and when I got to you... you made me feel what I was missing. So, this doesn't change anything. I feel like my storm is over and God has blessed me with not one mother but now two. Hell, with the type of baby daddy I got, I need all the help I can truly get." I laughed through my tears and my mom and Aubry joined in with my laughter.

"I can't believe that I didn't catch on to you, Aubry. We look a lot alike, and I noticed that you would never be super mean to me like you were with other students. I did feel like it was weird when you asked for my number and for us to meet up outside of school. I just didn't give it much thought because I still knew you personally, from being friends with my mom and always coming over to the house. Mom never gave me a solid reason why y'all had fell out. For a while I missed your presence and was thrilled when I saw that you were my teacher. Some of my classmates would say how me and Aubry looked alike because of our dimples and facial features. I see it clear now; I don't even want to know anything about my dad. I hate that he did what he did to you and my grandmother."

My knees started to burn so I stood up from the floor and sat right next to her.

"Y'all were good friends, I want y'all to reestablish that so we can all move forward with a healthy and great relationship." I was serious and hoped that they would take heed to what it is I was telling them. We sat and talked for a while until time passed by fast. I told my mom that I'd bring the kids by next weekend in hopes that Aubry would be here to properly introduce herself to her grandkids.

* * *

ARRIVING at Rodrik's momma's house had me sighing hard. Today had already been a long ass day and I didn't really want to deal with his bullshit today. Ever since he moved out and left the kids with toys and lots of gifts that I still didn't think he bought; he felt some type of way. I never kicked Rodrik out, but he made it seem as if I did.

My phone had rung, and I looked down at my caller ID and rolled my eyes hard. It was Nayvius calling. After he got me high, licked and fucked me so good and dipped on me like a thief in the night leaving me at his house turned me off really bad. I decided to not take things any further with his ass because red flags were clear as day about him and what all he did for a living.

Nayvius had this dangerous look in his eyes that made him attractive but also scared me to death. A part of me wanted to get deep with him and find out more while getting to know him. The way he looked at me and touched me, made me feel special. No other man has made me climax the way that Nayvius did. Good dick came with problems. The type of problems that could possibly have me down bad and I didn't need that. I realized after dealing with Rodrik for so long that us breaking up officially didn't hurt me as bad as it did because it was actually a burden off my damn shoulders.

I had two daughters and was trying to deal with Rodrik's bullshit when it came to co-parenting. I was mature enough and didn't have any hatred in my heart for Rodrik. I wanted to see him do good without me, Rodrik on the other hand, was bitter and wanted to make things harder than they needed to be. I needed things to be peaceful and I damn sure didn't want any baby daddy problems. So, with Nayvius, I didn't want to get too invested in him like I found myself being, all to get hurt. My daughter and school were my number one focus. I was the sole provider and they depended on me. I did not want to fail them.

I cleared Nayvius's call and blocked his number. For days he had been sending me all kinds of crazy text messages asking me why I was ignoring him. His last text sent a chill down my spine. He texted me late last night and just said "Bet". It was a simple one-word text, but it sounded like a threat. It was crazy how I missed him badly and wanted to just answer for him. I loved talking to him every day, he always put a smile on my face and asked about how the girls were doing, which was a plus for me.

Nayvius needed to understand like I should have made Rodrik understand a long time ago, that you couldn't just treat me any kind of way. Leaving me at his house like I was just some quick fuck was not gonna work for me. It took me a lot of courage to even see it through and go to his house that night. So, for him to move the way that he did with no explanation had me ready and willing to cut him off.

Rodrik walked out by himself from his mom's house, the look on his face already had me annoyed. He could have just walked my girls out of the house so I could go home already. I unbuckled my seat belt and got out of the car observing him walking up. He had his hair wild with a dingy shirt on like he had been laying around all day.

"Rodrik." I greeted him as he walked up, I looked around him to see if my kids were coming out of the house next. Looking down at my Kia Forte, I smiled. Besides all of the bullshit going on, I was grateful to finally have a car. My payments were low and affordable, so I wouldn't have to worry too much about going out of my budget for the following months. I was tired of getting on the bus, especially with my daughters. In L.A you saw some of the craziest things while riding the bus.

"I wanted to keep them for the night if that's okay with you." He licked his dry lips. I rolled my eyes because his antics were draining. I just wanted to pick my daughters up without an issue. Instead of telling him hell no, I decided to play it cool.

"That's fine with me." It was a big surprise to me as well.

"What made you want to keep them overnight?" I just had to ask out of curiosity.

"I'm their father, aren't I?" he asked sarcastically.

"Of course, you are Rodrik, it's just surprising to me that you are volunteering to keep them overnight. I know you like to play the game and jack off late at night with your gamer girl. I don't want my daughters apart of that or seeing it." I clapped back at him.

"They have their own room here, and my momma loves when her grandbabies are here. She's their real grandmother, not a foster grandparent." He was trying to hit below the belt with that jab as I tucked my lips, getting ready to curse his ass out.

"Me and my mom was talking earlier. I'm thinking about taking your hoe ass to court and handling my rights as a father. We can share custody and organize days that you get to keep the girls and I get to keep them. I don't want them around your thug ass boyfriend that walks around threatening niggas with guns." He gave me a knowing look as panic started to hit me. His words sounded rehearsed like his momma fed those words to him and gave him the idea of taking me to court.

"You don't even have a steady job or income. Nayvius is just a friend of mine, and he doesn't walk around with guns." I didn't know if the gun part was true, but I had to defend myself.

"He does! You were a coward ass bitch! Sending that nigga to give me a week to get out of our fuckin' house! Well, I'm gon' show you what the fuck I'm about Jaiden. You foul as fuck, been cheating on me the whole time then want to break up with me just because you catch me jacking off having game sex with a female that gives me more attention and interest then you."

I counted down to ten in my head and tried to calm myself down. I was ready to snap at the disrespect but didn't have enough energy to give it off to Rodrik.

"You damn right I couldn't give you the interest that she gives you! That gaming bitch doesn't get to see the bum ass nigga that I saw every day. Complaining about a McDonald's job that's part time, can barely help me with a light bill or put food on the fucking table! Rodrik, I swear if you disrespect me or play around with my daughters or even mistreat them, then I'll have Nayvius handle your bitch big kid ass!" I walked away from him and went to the driver's side of the door, opening it up.

"You better feed my daughters and if they tell me that you or your baldheaded trifling momma mistreated them while they are here tonight then Nayvius will be at your door with a big ass gun." His eyes grew wide with fear, disgusting me even further.

"Take me to court, I'm prepared for that shit to nigga." I

got into my car and started the engine and drove off. I was tired of people taking my kindness for weakness. I wanted to unblock Nayvius and curse his ass out for doing what he did to Rodrik. It was going to cause me problems if Rodrik really had the balls to take me to court.

I really didn't have the time to be in court fighting over custody but if he wanted to take it there. I'd be willing to do it for the safety of my daughters. Rodrik didn't want to have custody and I knew that deep down. He was okay with being a piss poor halftime father.

PRINCESS

"*Princess! Get yo funky ass up and clean up this house.*" *My mom banged hard on my bedroom door. I had a pounding headache from last night. All the liquor that I consumed along with the cocaine that I had sniffed up my nose had me feeling like my head was going to explode.*

I sluggishly picked up my phone that was next to my pillow and hit the lock button to light up the screen. I had a million missed calls from Histori. He called a hundred times a day relentlessly and sent me a million text messages. It was becoming hard to ignore him.

The longer I stayed here at my momma's house the more and more I yearned to just go back to him. Midas ruined me mentally and physically with the way he handled my body. Histori never made me explode back-to-back the way that Midas did. He hit places inside of me that I didn't know existed. I had flashbacks every day about the way that he felt inside of me. His large hands touching me and handsome face looking down at me.

I wanted him now more than ever and I hated myself more

and more for the decisions that I made eight years ago. I came up with several ways to get Midas back, but my greatest fear was losing Histori. I couldn't stop loving him for the life of me although I couldn't stand his ass for putting me in this position. No matter how bad Histori had hurt me, I didn't want the man dead. He was just somebody that I couldn't picture not existing in my life. Right now, I wanted nothing to do with him. At his mom's funeral when Midas took me with him, I saw that defeated look in Histori's eyes. Histori couldn't protect me which proved that Midas was indeed that nigga.

I wasn't happy with myself, to be honest. For years I've been lost, not really knowing which direction I wanted to take with my life. I loved fast money; I didn't have the patience to clock in at somebody's job or school. Plus, in my eyes it was a little too late. I needed a come up or a nigga that would fall in love with me and take care of me fully.

My eyes started to ring again and this time I went ahead and answered Histori call.

"What Histori?"

"Baby, you got me worried as fuck man. Where the fuck you at so I can come get you?"

"I'm exactly where I need to be nigga. Making my money and trying to do shit on my own this time. Your so fucking selfish Histori, I could've been with Midas years ago and married him and you had to bring your trifling ass back around, fucking things up for me."

"So, bitch you fucked that nigga? That nigga got you over there ready to just say fuck me when you was my bitch first? Princess, I love the fuck out of you Ma. I own you, I'm in your mind and body baby. You love me as well, I let you do you from time to time and you let me do me. It's how we have always been. I will never let you the fuck go P. I need to see

46

and protect you, that nigga Midas will kill you behind his bread. Tell me, where the fuck you at man." My phone started to beep, and I got excited seeing that after all this time Logic was calling me.

"I can't do this shit with you anymore Histori and I ain't fucking Midas. He doesn't want shit to do with me. He only wanted closure from the past. He did tell me though that he was going to kill you." I warned him and lied all in one. I knew that if I admitted to Histori that I fucked his brother that Histori would make my life a living hell. I also wanted to make sure that Histori protected himself and stayed safe. Damn, I was really in a fucked up position all because of this nigga and my stupid ass was still maintaining a certain level of loyalty to him when he didn't even deserve the shit.

"Princess... Please don't make a nigga have to start looking for you ma. You already know what the fuck I'm about. I will always fucking find you, baby girl."

"I know you will, Histori." I hung the phone up with tears rolling down my face. He always did find me and whenever he did, I always was so vulnerable and weak willing to do whatever just to go with him and feel like I was being saved. I could hear my mom walking around the house, stomping hard and talking shit about me. She was feening for a fucking argument. I didn't feel like going there with her today or any other day.

I had about five thousand dollars left after getting me a nice car. I was happy about my credit still being good, but a two thousand and twenty-three Audi truck hit me for a lot of money. Every month, my car note was close to eight hundred dollars with insurance, I would be paying damn near a thousand a month. My priorities were fucked up, but I loved having nice ass things.

I wouldn't dare be caught looking bummy or driving

something that was beneath me. I found a strip club that night I went out with Jaiden and was making a decent amount of money but still I needed a nigga to sponsor me. Hell, I wanted a nigga to sponsor me. Thinking about a nigga with money, placed my mind on the miss call that I had from Logic.

I looked down at my phone and weighed my damn options.

"Princess! Bitch, I know if I have to call your name one more time and you don't respond or come do what the fuck I say, yo hoe ass getting out my house today. Don't nobody lay up in this muthafucka half the day but me!" My mom pounded on my door again. She was so hot and cold with how she decided to act each day. One day she'd be laughing and joking with me then the next day she'd direct all her anger onto me and take out her frustrations with me by pointing out bullshit. I barely was even here for that matter, so I shouldn't have to clean up shit.

I got off the bed and opened up my room door glaring at her pathetic ass.

"You ain't the only one that be laid up in this bitch though. I get up and leave every day! The very first day that I decide to rest up before I go to work tonight you up in this bitch tripping, like I ain't breaking yo money hungry ass off to be up in this bitch. You only probably mad because daddy taking you through it! Kane don't do shit all day but bring hoes in and out of this bitch. You need to really chill the fuck out and let my pussy breathe cause you smothering my shit!" My mom's eyes turned into slits as she raised her hand to slap me.

I caught her hand and held on to her wrist tight as hell. Her eyes widened, I never thought about hitting my momma until now. I was really tired of her shit when she was the main cause for all my problems from the very beginning.

"You hoe ass, disrespectful, lazy ass, nasty, fat bitch! I knew from the moment I pushed you out of my good ass pussy that you were going to cause hell in my household. You a lil Ms. Can't ever get right kind of bitch. The only reason why I let you come back home is because I don't want to see ya dumb ass stranded out in the streets. I don't want ya death on my conscious. You ain't shit though, just like ya daddy ain't shit. From this day forward, you can die and the only thing that I will do is collect the life insurance that I have been paying on your behalf since you were two years old." She chuckled evilly and pulled out a cigarette from her bra.

"Get all your things and get the fuck up out of my shit. You got about thirty minutes flat." She blew smoke in my face and slammed the door for me. I could feel my chest constrict as the tears blurred my vision. Her hate speech shouldn't have affected me so bad since I was used to her violent rants. I just became overwhelmed with emotions because I really felt like I didn't have anyone solid in my corner anymore but Jaiden.

Jaiden had her family and her own issues to deal with, so I didn't expect her to solve my shit. Jaiden was a good ear to listen to all my bullshit but her solutions to my problems were stupid to me. I had Histori but his love came with terms and conditions. My father loved me to pieces, but he was in and out of jail, he wasn't dependable.

The words that my mom had spoken had me starting to believe that everything she had just said was true. I wasn't shit; I didn't have shit to really stand on. The man that I felt really loved me would never forgive me unless I pulled a miracle out of my ass.

I swallowed down my emotions and wiped the tears that

had fallen down my cheeks. Going into my small closet, I pulled out both of my suitcases and started packing my shit up to get the fuck up out of here for the last time.

My mom stuck to her word and when thirty minutes hit, she was back at the door telling me that my time was up. I had no destination in mind, I didn't want to argue with her any further because deep in my soul I was ready to lay hands on her.

I don't know why when I got to the door, I expected her to say something. Sometimes I wished that our relationship was better then what it was. I knew that I loved my mom despite her flaw ass actions. I knew that if something had happened to her that it would leave me hurt and distraught. What I couldn't do was kiss her ass. I felt that I had to speak my peace just in case this was my last time ever saying a thing to her let alone seeing her. There was no turning back from here. I would never let her hurt me with cruel words again.

I got to the front door and released it like it had burned me. Turning to my mom, she hit her cigarette and had the nerves to have a pleased smirk plastered on her face.

"Don't think about begging, ya daddy do that enough and I'm always the fool to accept him with open arms and love him with everything in me. I'm not doing the same for you, Princess. You not God's gift to mankind." Her left leg started to bounce. She was annoyed but not as hurt as I felt battling to express just exactly how I felt.

I saved her feelings for years I didn't want her to face the ugly truth. Right now, I wanted to hurt her just as much as she hurt me. She looked down on me like I wasn't shit, acted as if none of me was a product of her. I sniffed up the snot that dared to fall from my nose and allowed my tears of pain to fall.

"I love you Ma, and nah, I ain't fenna beg yo toxic selfish

ass. I can no longer blame you for how I turned out... just like you shouldn't blame me for pretending like you and daddy's relationship was perfect. You decided to stay, you was so wrapped up into him that you didn't care that your fourteen year old daughter was getting dick down by an eighteen year old right under your fucking nose. I got soul ties with a nigga I can't seem to get out of my system. The nigga all inside of my mental. When I try to leave him..." I wiped at my tears and swallowed the painful lump in my throat.

"I can't... it's like he got some voodoo over me, and I start feeling all guilty when deep down I know I shouldn't. I come back here for some sort of sanity, but you constantly kick me every single time I'm down. You don't encourage me or support me for the better. It's like you don't want to see me be better than you. Kane ain't no better than me but you constantly praise him and go into your purse to support any half ass fake dream he sells you. The last time I felt a little love from you was when I was that pretty little chubby girl with pigtails running after you. The older I got the more the love faded. I don't know what's in store for me, I don't even know my next move. I just know it gotta be my best move possible because I'm never turning back. I'll never come back to you or even acknowledge you. I hate you but I love you at the same time Ma." I gave her my back and opened the front door.

"Princess..." her voice cracked a little, I didn't turn around to face her. I didn't even want to hear whatever it was she had to say. I was already broken enough; my heart never had the time to repair itself. Shutting the door, it felt like I was closing up a chapter in my life that I would never try to read into again. My mom was one less toxic person in my life, now all I had to do was keep the same energy for Histori.

PRINCESS

I snorted another line of cocaine hoping that it would take my mind away from all of my problems. I sunk lower in the tub, letting the water come up to my neck. Grabbing the box of Newport 100's, I took one out of the pack and sparked it up. Inhaling deeply, I exhaled the smoke feeling good and calm.

I was happy to be inside of a nice big house that was supposed to have been something that I shared with my man Logic. He was never here, he never came home, and he didn't answer any of my calls or text messages for the past two weeks. Right now, I was just enjoying not having to hear my mom talk shit to me, and I felt relieved not getting any calls from Histori.

It hurt me, but I missed Histori and still worried about him, even though I shouldn't. I had attachment issues to him and the fear of never being able to see him again scared me, but it was also something that I knew I needed to do. I already had started to condition myself that I would never go back to fucking around with him. I desperately wanted to get my life together, but every time I turned around it seemed like I was sinking further away from who I used to be.

Histori and my mom were both selfish and they used me up until I didn't know how to use and navigate myself and my life properly. Sniffing cocaine became something normal for me to do. I ran to the drug because it made me feel free. It made me make my bad decision-making feel right. Cocaine was my crutch and now that I sat up in Logic's house with nothing to do but shop and cook meals for him to never come home and eat these meals. I started feeling more dependent on the drug to keep me company.

The best part of some of my days was calling Jaiden and hearing her talk positively to me. Jaiden loved me and she was a real ass friend, I felt like I didn't deserve her, but she never gave up on me. She kept telling me while Logic was gone that I needed to search my brain and figure out what it is that I wanted to do in life. Time was ticking, I was now in my thirties and hadn't established a real career for myself except stripping and getting a nigga to drop a bag on me.

Reaching over the tub with my hand, I felt around for my baggie of cocaine to take another hit of it. Suddenly the bathroom door opened, and I couldn't find the baggie fast enough as Logic walked in looking like a million fucking bucks. His eyes didn't land on me first, it went right to the bag of cocaine lying on the bathroom floor.

I wish like hell I could literally crawl underneath a rock and hide or maybe even die then to see him turning up his nose and finally looking up at me with so much disgust.

"The fuck is this shit about, Princess?" He tucked his hands inside of his denim jeans and tilted his head to the side a little.

"Ummm." Was all I could muster up. I jumped at the sound of him pushing the lid of the toilet seat down hard. He took a seat, and just shook his head. I had nothing to say because I had been caught. I was defeated, the only good thing about this is if he put me out, I had enough money saved up to get me a hotel for a couple of weeks. I could go find a club to strip at to double what I already had saved, if things got too bad for me then I would have to go back to Histori. That was something I didn't want to do but would rather do than to be living with my momma.

"So, I met my father for the first time. My real dad, he seem like a cool cat. I ain't really feel it when he revealed to me who the fuck he was. Then some major shit went down with one phone call that had me ready to ride for that nigga even though he had been missing my entire life. He declined my help, but I found out some other shit that had me stunned like a muthafucka too." I pushed both of my hands under the water and let my head rest against the wall as I listened to him talk.

I liked Logic a lot, to be young he was charming, caring, and smart as hell. I sometimes forgot that he was even in his early twenties.

"I went to go see about my real momma; she didn't want to explain shit to me. All she said was that she wasn't going to allow me or my father to ruin her life. To her understanding, she has no kids." He chuckled, but in his chuckle, you could hear his resentment and pain.

"I guess it wasn't even my dad's fault because he didn't know my momma was even pregnant with me. Bitches be really cold out here you feel me, Princess? I feel like you a cold ass bitch too. Underneath all that cold exterior, you got a heart, and you just want to be loved properly. Shit, you probably don't even know what the fuck you want and that's okay to. You were dealt a fucked up deck of cards, you keep shuffling them bitches trying to see when you gone be able to have the right deck and get ahead in life. With me… I'm young and I got a lot of shit ahead of me for the future. I knew from the moment I saw you, that I was digging you. You thick as fuck, got a pretty ass face and even though you make dumb ass decisions… I know you smart, you a hustler like me, and sometimes you can even be a fast-ass talker. When I'm around you, I can't think to straight cause I'm sexually, mentally, and physically attracted to you. It's like some sort of magnetic pull you got over me. Besides all of that, I won't let you play me like a sucker ass nigga. My father is Midas, Princess. You fucked on him, and your ex-nigga kidnapped his momma. I thought that when my father revealed that he fucked on you and how you use to be his bitch too… I thought that it would make me speed here and kick you out on your ass. What good would that be, when I still got feelings for you. Ain't nobody there for you, that shit evident as fuck. Fucking with my father is the past for you, but shoving the same shit that I sell in big quantities is a no go for me Ma. I can't fuck with you off that shit. You fucking up your beauty… bags under your eyes, you losing weight and all that Princess. I can't fuck with you on some serious shit if you on that white devil baby."

My heart rate sped up at so many things that he had just said. He said a whole mouthful and surprisingly I didn't give a fuck about Histori at this exact moment because he was stupid as hell to kidnap Midas mom. Ms. Wellington was a sweet ass lady and didn't deserve that. As I looked into Logic's hazel eyes, I saw a good man with a heart of gold trying to give me a fair chance. Sure, he wasn't perfect but something inside of me told me that he was worth it.

"If I go get help, would you still be willing to give me a chance?" he licked his thick sexy lips and nodded his head up and down.

"I will Ma, I'll even help you figure out what you want to do instead of stripping. Help you get a job and feel good about yourself. That's what you need, real shit. I'll keep it real at all times, you know I do my thang when it comes to bitches because they come a dime a dozen. In my head, I don't belong to anybody until they can prove to me that they belong fully to me. I ain't been on no faithful shit with you because you showed me in the beginning that you weren't gon' be on that with me. If you really serious though, Princess... show me that shit and I will show you too." Logic stood up and walked up to me and held his hand out.

I slowly stood still feeling the rush and adrenaline from the cocaine. He sobered me up with everything he had said and now I was feeling super emotional. My hands started to shake as I slowly got out of the bathtub, standing in front of him naked with water dripping off of me.

Logic pulled me in for a tight hug and I needed it, I felt myself buckle in his arms as he made sure to hold me up and keep his arms wrapped around me tightly. Sobbing right into his chest, I let out years of pain and frustration. All the times I had been let down and getting my hopes up high all for them to be let down. Years of staying with the same man that could never love me how I loved him.

Logic didn't even have to offer what it was he was offering. I wanted to be saved but I knew the first step was saving myself. Everything happened for a reason, I couldn't even wrap my head around the fact that Logic was Midas' son. I felt dirty, I literally slept with an entire family and wasn't aware. The more I look at Logic the more I could see the similar features and resemblance from Midas.

After hugging Logic for about ten minutes letting out my tears and pain. We both got in the shower together. He scrubbed my body from head to toe and I returned the favor. I watched him flush my cocaine down the toilet and we got in bed together. We laid in bed while he searched for rehab places that would work for me. The fact that he was willing to help me spoke volumes, even if me and Logic didn't work out, I would keep him as a friend for life. I hoped that we worked out because he was truly a good person besides the other flaws he had.

Logic held me and he opened up telling me that his real name was Diamond. He hated the name Diamond because it sounded feminine to him. He also told me how once Ms. Wellington got better, he was going to let his father train him and teach him more. It was a relief that Ms. Wellington was okay, Logic stated that she was in a coma to heal and reduce the swelling from around the right side of her brain.

My mind went back to Histori and how evil and self-absurd he had to be to actually go through with kidnapping an elderly woman. The calls and texts from him had stopped and I wondered if he was already dead. A part of me felt sad for his death but he kept eating away at the beast in Midas. Histori would get what he deserved even if it sounded sick of me. A part of me would always love him, I had good memories and a lot of bad memories with that man. I was connected to him for years and had grown accustomed to his fucked-up ways just like I did with my mom. My brother Kane has been calling me for two weeks now and each time I declined his calls.

Now that Logic was here telling me all of this, I decided that it would be great to give my brother a call back and see what it was that he wanted. We didn't have the best relationship because we always argued, but just like anybody else that dogged me out, I loved him. He was my blood.

I was happy for Logic, he really seemed excited about knowing who his father was. I would be excited too if Midas was my dad. He was wealthy, smart, and truly one of a kind. That man had the Midas Touch when it came to any challenge. I was blessed to experience his raw uncut love once and now that I'm laid up with his son, it made me feel like God gave me a second chance to experience his love again.

Once Logic had fallen into a deep sleep, I got out of bed and grabbed my phone. Walking out of the bedroom, I went into the living room to sit on the couch. I didn't know why I was so nervous about calling him back. Kane never called me, whenever he did call, it was to always talk shit.

"Kane." I said his name calmly, waiting for him to say something back.

"Princess, I'm sorry sis…." Panic alarmed me, my stomach started to turn and do flips.

"What's going on Kane?" I heard him sniffle hard. He breathed loudly in the phone then took in another deep breath.

"Dad is back in jail for assaulting momma." I dropped my head and held the phone tight.

"I'm going to put some money up to try to get him bail but he haven't had his hearing yet. I figured that I'd talk to momma but she's in the hospital healing."

"Why would daddy hurt her like that Kane!" I got pissed thinking about my mom laid up in a hospital and being hurt. I knew that they argued and sometimes they even fought, but my dad never hurt my mom in a bad way. Whenever they did fight it was blows from my mom and my dad pushing her hard to get her off of him.

"He hurt her because of everything she had been doing to you. It's a part of my fault too. I shouldn't have been a scary ass nigga. I should have protected you as my little sister. We all failed you. I knew that Histori was sick for liking you at a young age, shit me and him were grown. Then you fell in love with him, and momma turned a blind eye to it. Pops didn't know shit about it because he was too busy in the streets making money. If pops had known though he would've killed Histori himself. I couldn't hold that shit on my conscious any longer so after Midas basically kidnapped me to lead him to Histori. I came back home and told Pops everything." My heart was beating out of my chest right now.

"What did you tell him Kane? We all know how bad momma talks to me. Daddy even checks her for the shit, and he has left her a couple of times for treating me wrong. So, what could be so bad this time?"

"She got pregnant a couple of times by Histori. She's been in love with him too. In her sick-ass mind, she figured if you keep messing with him that it would keep him around her too. At the same time, she hated you because he loved you instead of her. This time though, she kept the last baby that she got pregnant with. The doctor said the baby survived the brutal beating that daddy gave her. I told dad that and I told him everything else about how and when you and Histori started fucking around." Kane's voice broke and he started to cry as I softly wept holding the phone in my hands.

"Pops told me that he doesn't want shit to do with me no more. He said that I failed to protect you when he wasn't around and he's right about that, Princess… I'm so fucking sorry. Momma wants me out of her house, and she said she's done with me for telling pops everything. I can't have you turn on me either, our family is so fucked up, I just was trying to make shit right."

"Why she hate me so fucking much, Kane?" I really wanted to know but probably would never get the answers.

"Because you're you, baby." I froze and looked at Logic standing at the end of the hallway. He walked all the way in, I tried to slow down the tears that were falling from my eyes, but they wouldn't ease up. He kneeled right in front of me and looked me in the eyes as I held onto the phone listening to Kane cry.

"Your mom is insecure for whatever reasons. She feels threatened by you and it confuses her how no matter what she dishes out to you, it doesn't break you fully. It might stumble you and keep you on the same destructive path, but that shit doesn't break you when she has already been broken as a woman. I bet she avoids eye contact with you, she probably never smiles when she sees you. She doesn't include you in conversations and when others mention you, she changes the subject because she can't bear to hear someone speak positively about you. She ignores you and gives you backhanded compliments because she never wants you to feel good about yourself. Time has passed her; she has gotten older while you still have time on your side. Somewhere deep inside of her, she loves you... but she has to get rid of the hate she has for you. That shit don't happen overnight baby. So, until it happens, you gotta give her space and still love and respect her from a distance so you can get yourself healthy and rid yourself of the toxic behaviors that you have grown accustomed to." Logic picked up my hand and kissed the back of it, making my heart flutter. He had eased my hurt that fast, and I suddenly realized how soon I should have let go of Histori and my mom.

"You right baby." I nodded my head and wiped the last set of tears that escaped my eyes.

"I don't know who that is Princess but he right as fuck. Momma always been a hater when it comes to you. She loved to brag when you were stripping telling people that was all you'd ever be. I know you can be more. Shit, she hated you the most when you were going to school and doing something positive for yourself. Prove her wrong and if you let me... this time around. I want to be there for you." I smiled weakly.

"I'd like that Kane. We never had a real good sibling bond, but I would love to establish one." He agreed and I told him about going to rehab and getting myself together. We got off the phone and Logic was spreading my thick thighs apart with a look of hunger evident in his eyes.

"What you doing baby." I moaned at the feeling of his beard tickling my thighs. The feel of his soft, thick licks kissing my inner thighs had me instinctively opening my legs wider for him.

"I want to suck all of your problems, pain, and hurt right from your pussy. Make you mine and watch you become the woman that I know you can become. All this shit gone take time, and we can figure it all out together. I want to see you happy. Fuck treating you like a princess; I'm giving you Queen treatment… just don't fuck it up."

"Ohhhhh! Fuck!" he spread my pussy lips by shaking his head from side to side. My clit started to throb, and he started licking it real steady then dipping his tongue down to my soaked center. I closed my eyes and got lost in ecstasy enjoying the feeling of Logic loving on me.

MIDAS

hree months later

I HATED BEING AT HOSPITALS, every time I entered one, all I
could think about was my father. They couldn't save him;
they gave us hope and told us everything that we wanted to
hear, all for him to succumb to his gunshot wounds and die
hours later. I didn't blame them; I blamed the niggas that did
what they did to him. Now I sat inside of this cold ass
hospital room, legs bouncing because my nerves were bad,
looking over at my mom sleeping like she was at peace.

The room smelled like antiseptics, a little bitter, with
undertones of the artificial fragrance contained in the soaps
that the nurses used constantly upon entering the room. My
mom was strong, they removed half of the right side of her
brain and skull, preserving it so that it can heal properly. The
bullet went through her cheek and out of her skull. The right
side of her face was fractured so she was looking at several
surgeries.

Reconstruction of the right side of her face was needed and it was a good thing that the bullet went straight through her skull so there were no bullet fragments left inside, just injured vessels. She came out of the coma, but they put her into an induced coma from her getting worked up when she did finally wake up. I sat waiting for the anesthesiologist to come in, today was the day they took her off the meds that kept her resting all day.

Two taps at the door got my attention as I sat up, fixing my posture. This had to be the anesthesiologist coming in finally and now I was nervous praying everything went well.

"Okay, so I'm just going to check her vitals life functions. That includes her heart rate, and rhythm. Breathing, blood temperature, and body fluids. I also want to see if she is in too much pain before I lower the dosage. We are winging her off slowly so that we can start removing a couple of the tubes."

I licked my lips staring at Aubry in amazement. She was my mother's doctor and anesthesiologist, which had me really interested in knowing more about her. She had a lot of titles under her belt. From the looks of it, I could tell that she was a hard-ass worker like myself. People like us always stayed busy, never making time personally to do the things that we needed to do to stay in tune with ourselves.

Aubry switched off with my mom's old doctors because she had to fly out to tend to a family emergency. I was shocked to see Aubry a month ago. She treated me like a stranger as if she wasn't still one of my professors at my college. I hadn't forgotten about our little encounter.

"Did the test results come back in yet for the liquid that was coming out of her nose?" I sat up a little further really taking Aubry in. I mean this woman was beautiful with lots of sex appeal. Even with scrubs on I could see all of her curves. She had her shoulder length hair pressed straight with a part down the middle. I loved the dark brown freckles that were splattered across the bridge of her nose, forehead, and cheekbones. I even noticed three little moles underneath her right eye.

Aubry had chinky eyes, light brown skin and when she opened her mouth to speak her deep-dish dimples sunk into her cheeks and the gap between her perfectly aligned teeth complimented her all-white teeth.

"Yes, and I have good news about that!" She smiled, making me smile right back at her.

"It was brain fluid which is good because if it was spinal fluid that would be a big red flag. Spinal fluid would make us aware that she has an infection somewhere in her brain. Brain fluid is okay, it's better for it to drain out, then stay in before we perform another surgery placing the right side of her brain and skull back in."

"When will that surgery take place?" I don't know why but I felt the urge to stand up and get a little closer to her.

"Umm, well... I can't give you a date... we have to see how fast the vessels that were struck heal. Everything is a process and it's up to Ms. Wellington. First, we would like to see her off of the meds that has her in an induced coma. We want to make sure she has her memory, and we also want to see what all is infected. So far, we know that she doesn't have bullet fragments in her eyes."

"Why is her eye so red?"

"Because its blood, the right side of her face was fractured causing blood vessels to burst. The blood in her eyes will clear up with time." I nodded my head and watched her walk up to the machines that were hooked up to my mom. She pulled out her clipboard and pressed buttons on several machines. Every couple of seconds Aubry would write down a few words onto her clipboard. My eyes traced down to her wide hips and round ass, I had to tell myself not to try to make a move. I just couldn't help how drawn in I was with this woman.

"Understand Midas that your mom is older... Her body needs time to heal and adjust to the injuries she has sustained." I nodded my head and got quiet letting her focus on caring for my mom. Running my hands through my kinky coils that badly needed done, I sighed and looked over at my mom.

I hadn't got any proper rest since I got her, and I haven't eaten a good meal. I snacked here and there and filled my lungs up with lots of weed smoke to help me cope through this new change. I robotically handled the things that needed to be handled as far as work goes. I practically lived here at this hospital night and day.

"That'll be all for the day, Mr. Wellington." I looked up and smiled at Aubry who was now looking at me with concern.

"Now I'm back to Mr. Wellington. I like when you call me Midas." She blushed and looked away from me. When she gave me her eyes again, there was a bashful look evident in her eyes.

"I try to remain professional at all times. You look like you could use some help as well right now."

"Is that right?" I licked my lips and stretched out a little in the chair that I was sitting in.

"What kind of help Aubry? Or should I say Dr. Jackson." She giggled lowly; I hadn't missed the new light in her eyes. When I saw her months ago in that classroom it looked like her light had been dimmed by something. Given that she had a hard past, I knew that it could be one of the reasons, now she was more perky and smiling like something had changed in her life. I hoped that it wasn't a nigga that had got involved, I thought my touch would be enough to hold her over until she gave me a chance to really get to know her.

"You look like you could use a real meal, you've lost weight. The color of your skin has changed a little too which means you're probably dehydrated. Your hair looks horrible, you don't look like the man that came into my classroom months ago with so much arrogance." She smirked right back at me; our exchange was real light, but it felt powerful.

"I suppose I do need help Aubry. I need a hug too. My mom always gave me the best hugs, since she's been here, I haven't gotten one. I'm hungry and I only let my momma touch my head to fix my hair." We both remained silent for a couple of seconds until I broke the silence.

"I think I would be willing to trust you with a meal and your hands in my head. That's if you're able to trust yourself around me." I raised my brows, and she laughed hard this time. A real laugh, that made me feel real good. She snapped her head back, her dimples sunk deep into her cheeks, she didn't hold back or try to quiet down. The laugh came straight from her stomach and spread throughout the room that we had occupied. It was the most beautiful sound that I have heard in a long time.

Aubry sounded pure, clear, and melodic. Like an angel had touched her voice box making her deliver such a beautiful sound. It was contagious and although I truly felt like I had nothing to laugh about, I joined her. Her laugh faded away and she wiped the tears of joy off her cheeks.

"You real smooth and corny Midas. I can use the company as well. I don't mind helping you, I know how to recoil hair and braid. If you are cool with eating leftovers then you're in luck tonight because I cooked salmon nuggets, mashed potatoes, and asparagus last night. You can come and hang with me for a little while but not too long because I have to be right back here at six in the morning."

Heat coursed through my veins just thinking about being in her personal space where she laid her head. We were making progress but as a man, I already knew that I had to take things slowly.

"That sounds like a plan, I guess it's safe for me to get your number." I never felt nervous conversing with a woman a day in my life, but Miss Aubry had me thinking before speaking. I didn't want to say the wrong thing to make her shy away from me or think that I was just like every other man trying to get between her thick thighs because I wasn't.

"Give me your phone." I dug in my pocket and handed my phone over to her. I watched her tap at my screen and then her phone rang.

"I'm storing you in now, Mr. Wellington." The way my last name rolled off of her tongue had me bricking up. I watched her walk away and had to look away. In due time Aubry Jackson would be something more to me other than a good friend. Something told me that she would be the woman to take my deck of cards in add the card of love.

I got up and moved to the chair closer to my mom. Grabbing her hand, I kissed the back of it and smiled down at her.

"I been trying to talk to God ma. It's been hard because I've been keeping the nigga that did this to you locked away. I want to live right like you been begging me to. Have you some grandkids and give this love thing another chance. One thing you taught me was patience and I've been having that when it comes to you because I know it's going to take time for you to heal. I just miss you so much it hurts. I can't wait until you fully woke up and can get on my case. You need to curse Zori out too. Can you believe she had a kid by me? My son grown as hell ma, but he looks just like me." I stopped talking when her heart rate increased.

"I know, I know but calm down Ma. I don't want you getting worked up right now when I gotta go get ready for a date in a couple of hours." I chuckled at that. Aubry was smooth as hell asking me to come to her house.

"I need you to heal and get better so you can meet this woman that got me all nervous like a straight B word." I stood and kissed her on the forehead. I looked at her for a couple more minutes then walked out of the room feeling like today was a good day and tonight would feel even better.

I got home and showered and dressed down in a pair of black sweats with a white tee and black hoodie. Before I left the house, I went to the backyard to smoke a blunt and call Shooter. Shooter had men watching over Histori, it wasn't much watching that they needed to do because I had that nigga hanging by his wrist suspended up in air. He hadn't eaten shit but one bottle of Ensure and two bottles of water a day.

I beat his ass multiple times and used him as a punching bag to build my cardio up.

"What's good." Shooter spoke into the phone.

"Shit, getting ready to go on a date." I smiled. Shooter chuckled into the phone, and I joined him.

"Don't tell that nigga Goof yet. Nigga gone bag on me for an hour straight." I laughed knowing exactly how Goof was.

"Nah, that nigga don't want to hear shit about no dates. He still salty about that girl cutting him off cold. Nigga talking about popping up at that girl crib to make her unblock him." I shook my head because this was some new shit for Goof. He didn't chase women and after his Ex Vanessa, all he did was stick and move with females like me.

"She gon' come around, females love playing hard to get.

Just got to apply that Midas touch to them and it's a wrap for the tough act that they try to display."

"That's for y'all niggas that love shit will never be in the cards for me. I got favorites and females that I hit and never call again. I tell every woman that I will never be faithful."

"You say that now until you meet your match. How is that nigga doing." I got to the point of why I was really calling.

"Begging with the little bit of strength he has."

"Good, as soon as my mom wakes up then his lights can be cut."

"It's done." With saying nothing else, I ended the call. I took the sims card out of the burner flip phone and broke it in half. The phone would be disposed of, even though we talked in code, you could never be too sure.

Going to the key rack that I kept by the back door that led to my three-car garage, I decided to take my Tahoe truck. Aubry lived in Long beach so the drive from my house would take about twenty minutes since there was no traffic. This would be the first night in months that I spent free time away from the hospital and school to go do some leisure type shit, so I considered this a date.

AUBRY

J greased my body with my handmade oil and put
on something cozy. Looking myself over in the
mirror, I hoped that what I had on wasn't too much or less of
what Midas expected. Midas was something else but very
charming and handsome as hell. The way that he talked and
carried himself made any woman want to get close and know
more. It was rare that you come across a man confident and
assertive of themselves.

The older you get the more you want to get right to the
point. It was clear that Midas and I had a strong attraction to
one another. He was well established and so was I, besides
my issues. I was forty-three years old and hadn't laid with a
man since my husband had died and that had been too many
years to even try to count. I didn't have friends, the one real
friend that I did have was Cherry. It was hard for me to trust
people but when I did, and they broke that trust, it made
things very hard for me to forgive.

I still loved Cherry, but I could never fully trust her again.
She made things hard for me and I take accountability
because I could've just told Jaiden that I was her mother. I

just didn't know what all Cherry had said to her. It was a sticky situation, but I was happy that it was finally revealed. A lot of time was wasted, and I really didn't know where to begin with Jaiden. I prayed on it every day since she found out and these past couple of months, Jaiden and I talked on the phone at night every day like we were old best friends trying to catch up from lost time.

I shook my head as I stared at my thick thighs and decided that I needed to cover up a little more. I didn't want to make it too obvious that I wanted Midas big hands all over me. I just wanted and needed some form of intimacy. In today's society things were changing. The old generation of men were learning from the new generation of men. It seemed like the masculinity of black men was fading away. Either a man dogged a woman out or wanted an open relationship. The new wave was the polygamous lifestyle which was something I would never in my life try. Men wanted to be called men but act like women and gossip more than them. Last but not least there were so many down low men, and undercover niggas that were too scared to live in their truth while some of their favorite rappers glorified the lifestyle.

I missed my husband, Alex, he was such a good caring man and loved on me with every ounce of him with no holding back. I worked by choice because I always wanted to contribute to my household. Alex still provided and paid every bill that we had. When he died, I couldn't bear staying in the house we shared so I rented it out and moved to a nice area in Long Beach, right next to the beach. I slept peacefully at night knowing I was close to the water. Plus, my apartment had all the amenities that a single woman needed.

Now that I had grandkids, I couldn't wait to give them more and help Jaiden out as much as I could. I had money saved so I stopped counting. I didn't live above my needs, and I saved money like I was going to one day run out of it. I kept my nails and hair done once every three weeks. Once every couple of months, I'd go online and shop for clothes because I didn't have the patience to hit the mall like I was in my twenties.

I went to my dresser and picked out a new pair of winter pajamas that I had been wanting to wear. The long thermal pants had candy canes and reindeer on them, the thermal shirt was identical to the pants. I shook my head and thought the look might be corny. I hadn't struggled with what the hell to put on in years because I really wasn't trying to please anyone but my damn self. I guess you can say I adapted to being alone. I enjoyed the simple things like getting off of work from a long day. Going into my kitchen and cooking a good meal, then sitting in my cozy living room burning candles while sipping wine while watching a good show or reading a good urban book. My off days consisted of me making oil perfumes and body butters along with body scrubs and soaps. I had dreams of starting a business out of that if I ever allowed myself to have some free time.

I entertained myself, and also took myself out on dates alone so I won't go into a deep depression. I didn't do the self-pity thing or get in my feelings about being alone. I was fine with my solitude. I grew up going from home to home and had been treated like dog shit until I was old enough to stand on my own two feet.

I still stood looking down at my open dresser, staring down at the matching pair of pajamas. Biting at my bottom lip, feeling annoyed with my own decisiveness, I picked the matching pair up and closed my drawer. Fuck it, I was going to cover my body. The last thing I wanted Midas to think was that I was desperate. I already embarrassed myself months back in the classroom alone with him having an orgasm from just his simple touch.

"Can't be too corny, you only retwisting his hair and feeding him some food I thought out loud. I always talked to myself and didn't see anything wrong with it. Call it crazy but even when I asked myself a question, I answered that same question. I never led myself in the wrong direction.

Midas didn't know what he sparked in me months ago in that classroom. I left the school campus and sped all the way home that day, pulling out all kinds of dildos and vibrators. I played with myself until I grew disgusted with watching porn and making myself cum over and over again. I imagined Midas doing all kinds of things to my body. I wanted to feel him so bad, and he was the blame. He came on to me strong, with all of his masculinity.

I loved a man that could rock a suit with pure confidence, his breath smelled good and soon as he had walked inside of my classroom, his scent took over the entire room. He was tall and in shape, it had to be a weird obsession because his handsome face popped into my head during random times of the day. Even with his mom in the hospital, I kept things professional. I been wanting to offer my helping hand with support for him.

He was there night and day by himself, there were two men that came to bring him food and visit with his mom which also told me that he was single. No woman ever accompanied him at the hospital. Midas had a ladies' man look to him. Just from his looks and persona alone I knew he had women all over him or a long roster of women. Which was why all I had to offer him was a good friendship. It just seemed like we would vibe good.

I also saw that he needed a woman's touch in his life. He had at least lost fifteen to twenty pounds and his hair was a

73

mess on top of his head. He was a momma's boy, so he let himself go since his mother was in the hospital. Just as I went to pull down my fuzzy pink pajama shorts, my doorbell rang, and my stomach automatically started to tighten. I got so nervous that I started to pass gas, it was better that I let it all out now than to get in the same space as him and slip up and let it go in front of him.

I opened my legs while standing and fanned between my legs so whatever smell could go away. Giggling to myself, I went back up to my dresser, to pick up my lighter and light up my scented candles that smelled like my body oils. By the time I finished lighting my candles my doorbell rang again. My nerves were jittery, and I felt excited to even have company at my door.

Nervously, I walked out of my room shutting the door behind me. As I walked down the hallway, I eyed every part of my house to make sure nothing was out of place. I lived in a two-bedroom apartment, it was the perfect size for me, not too small and not too big. My house was clean and smelling good. Passing my couch, I looked at the coffee table, I had already placed a small bucket with all of my hair supplies that I would use on Midas.

I counted down from three in my head and opened the door to Midas standing there with a box of Forever pink roses that I could tell cost a pretty penny. A big smile crossed my face, I refrained from shedding a tear or two because I hadn't had a man buy me roses in forever.

"Thank you." I blushed and inhaled his scent. Midas nodded his head smoothly; he looked different dressed down in sweats and a hoodie. He had to lean down a little to enter through the front door. Shutting the door behind him, he took his hoodie off, and I just stood there stuck staring at his abs and smooth brown skin. Straightening his shirt, he hung his hoodie on the coat rack and then approached me reeking of confidence. My stomach did summersaults as I licked my glossed-up lips and waited in anticipation for what was to happen next. Midas still hadn't uttered a word. He pulled me up against him and hugged me tightly. Stunning me, his hands left my lower back and cuffed the bottom of my ass, giving it a light squeeze he pecked me in the nook of my neck and then inhaled sharply. Pulling back Midas stared down into my eyes, I instinctively stood on my tippy toes, struggling to place my arms around his neck.

"I been waiting to do this for a while now." His deep voice murmured lowly.

"Do what?" I got caught up in his gaze, his deep set of brown eyes had me mesmerized. The patch of beard hair on his chin shined like he put some oil in it, I wanted to grab it and rake my fingernails through it. His two-toned brown full lips turned upwards into a smirk.

"Hold you in my arms, so you can feel my touch again." He bent down and pecked me on the lips.

"You really straightforward huh?"

I giggled as I moved out of his arms feeling myself growing hot all over.

"I am when I need to be." His light chuckle was deep and smooth.

"You look good baby, pajama shorts and all. I wished you put on pants, your thighs…" He paused as his eyes dropped low and focused on my thick ass thighs. My thighs weren't firm at all, but I loved the body I was in. I had dimples and cellulite covering my thick ass thighs. If he didn't like them then ol' well.

"They thick as fuck…" He touched at the top of my fuzzy shorts and let his fingertips graze my exposed thigh. "They oiled down, you smell good as hell, I know you want me between your legs... To do my hair. Don't want you standing after the long work shift." He smirked and walked towards my sectional couch. When he said that I wanted him between my legs my mind instantly went right into the damn gutter. Now my clit was thumping hard, I was turned on from the moment he gave me that pretty box of roses.

"You want me to warm your food up now?" I watched him sit on the floor.

"Yea, my stomach has been cursing me out since I left home. Thank you." I walked off to the kitchen and pressed hit the button on the microwave to heat his food up. I planned his arrival; I made his plate before I got in the shower and put it in the microwave so it could be ready for him. I already ate soon as I got home. I never bought food from the hospital. It was always overpriced and nasty. I enjoyed my home-cooked meals. It was rare for me to go spend money and eat somebody else's cooking when I loved my own.

I brought Midas his plate of food with some of my homemade lemonade. He thanked me and wasted no time digging in. I grabbed up my hair bucket and sat down right behind him and started parting, greasing and re coiling his hair which was easy. His grade of hair was thick and cotton soft, it easily curled up like it was trained from the coils his mom put in his hair. I loved the fact that his hair smelled good like he washed it in the shower before coming to me. Most men didn't wash or maintain their hair properly while refusing to cut it. When Midas finished eating, he sat the plate on the coffee table and thanked me again for the meal. We sat silent listening to music with the tv off. Next thing I knew, he picked up one of my feet and started to slowly massage it.

I wanted to moan the way his strong hand handled my toes and feet; he rotated my foot then took his hands and squeezed around my ankle applying the right amount of pressure. He took his time on my right foot then made it over to my left foot. I don't know why, tears welled up in my eyes. I guess it was a sweet gesture.

After work my feet always hurt the worst no matter how comfy my shoes were. When I got to work, I never really sat down, I basically stood my whole ten-hour shift. I didn't want to compare him to my husband Alex, but this reminded me of him. He always catered to me no matter how tired he was from working. We catered to each other.

"That feels so good, Midas." I sighed, parting and adding grease to his scalp.

"Your hands in my head feel good too." He turned a little and looked up at me. His brows bunched up together as he eyed me intently.

"What's wrong?"

"I just haven't been touched intimately since my husband. It's been years, and it feels great." I lowered my eyes back to his head, but he kept his eyes glued to me. Maneuvering his body until he was on his knees between my legs with his hands on each side of me, he leaned in and kissed me. His breath tasted like the strawberry lemonade I made for him. Midas lips were chilled and soft. As soon as his tongue entered my mouth, I couldn't hold back the moan that escaped my lips into his mouth. I relaxed as Midas hands massaged my thighs. He pulled away from me with hooded low eyes filled with lust.

"Nah, I gotta stop and not take it there with you. I need you to open up more and when the time comes, I want every part of your body, including your mind so I can know how to read it when you don't tell me what I'm trying to figure out." He left me panting, hungry for more of him. My nipples ached and now I wished he wasn't between my thighs because my clit kept pulsating. I could feel how wet I was without even touching myself. Keeping my pride intact, I searched his eyes to be sure if he was serious about pulling away.

"When I look at you… It feels like I'm getting a glimpse of meeting God. I've been thinking hard on changing some things attached to myself, Aubry. Things that I'm not proud of, things that my mom has been begging me for too. A person can want something for you, but you have to want it for yourself. A part of me feels that change more and more each time I lay eyes on you. My momma said it and wants it for me, and now that I see you, I want it for myself and for you." He leaned down and pecked me on each thigh.

"Why do you want it for me?"

"I see a story in your eyes. I'm an honest man, I won't lie… from the classroom interaction with you, I became curious, I saw so much pain and anger in your eyes. I looked into you, to see what would come up. The things I saw, no woman should have to ever experience. If that nigga was alive, I'd find him and kill him dead." A darkness took over his face and I could tell he was serious. I wasn't surprised that Midas looked into me. Paid men did some of the craziest things.

"So, you live a double life?" I picked up on all of this change talk he was speaking of and how he mentioned seeing God in me.

"Something like that, as far as work life."

"What about women? Do you have a lot of them?"

"No, I don't have time for them. I haven't had sex since I found out about my son. My ex hid the fact that she was pregnant when we were younger. She gave my boy away without telling me. I'm trying to get to know him and the kind of man he is. That shit still fucks with me. I still try to give everyone the benefit of the doubt but that shit with Zori and one of my close friends fucked me up." He got up off his knees and sat right next to me. Throwing his long arm around me, I leaned into his chest and relaxed since we were conversing. I no longer felt nervous and shy. It felt like we had been friends for a very long time.

right next to me. Throwing his long arm around me, I leaned into his chest and relaxed since we were conversing. I no longer felt nervous and shy. It felt like we had been friends for a very long time.

"Zori slept with a close friend of yours?" I pressed for more information.

"Yea, I found out about my son and then found out about Zori and my friend. Before I knew about it all, I was close with both of them. I even overlooked the fact that Zori was stealing money from me."

"Oh, hell no!" I sat up as Midas chuckled at my reaction.

"Hell yea..." this time he laughed a little harder.

"Shieetttt.... She need her ass beat." I stated, seriously.

"She probably do, but I wasn't tripping too hard, I had got hurt a lil worse before with my son girlfriend." He shrugged like what he was saying wasn't some heavy shit.

"Wait... Midas! So, you telling me you were fucking your son girlfriend?"

"No, I was once in love with her. Thought she would be my wife; I proposed to her and didn't touch her sexually because I thought she was a virgin and shit. I end up getting set up by my brother who is responsible for shooting my momma, holding her hostage to extort me for money. She ran off with my brother before that almost leaving me for dead. I found out that she was my brother's girlfriend first and that she wasn't a virgin..." He chuckled and shook his head as he looked down into my eyes.

"I'm skipping around because it all ain't in order. Long story short when my brother kidnapped my mom and called me... I was having a sit down with my son, it was my first time meeting him. I mentioned her name and my son said that she was his girlfriend."

"So that bitch basically fucked the whole family. Wow,

now this some piping hot tea." I fanned myself like I was burning up.

"What happened to your friend that was sleeping with your baby momma?"

"He's dead." Midas stated flatly, not blinking an eye. A chill ran down my spine because the way he said it made me feel like he did.

"Careful on what you ask me. I feel like I can trust you, Aubry. I said a lot a couple of seconds ago and I notice you ain't mention calling the police for my brother who shot my mom." I was green but I wasn't that green.

"Well, I didn't mention the police because I figure he's probably dead or on his way to being dead." I smiled shyly and Midas let a deep rumble of laughter escape his mouth that serenaded me instantly.

"I like the fuck out of you. My momma gonna like you too. A lot of people don't like to put two and two together. So, since I'm telling you so much, have you reached out to your daughter?"

"Yea I have, we actually talk every day now." I smiled thinking about Jaiden, she was such a sweet girl.

"Damn you know all my business." I play-punched him and he acted like I really hurt him.

"I gotta know everything about you, especially if I'm planning on making you mine." I blushed hard and told him to get back on the floor so I could finish his hair.

I started back up on his hair and we talked about everything under the sun. Our conversation flowed effortlessly, we laughed, got serious, and even gave each other advice. I finished up Midas hair and went to warm up some more leftovers for him and me. When he left my house, it was midnight and I wished we had more time to chill. I had work early and he didn't want to miss a night from staying with his mom. I swooned when he pulled me close at my door before leaving. He held me so close to his chest, my body up against his. Holding me tight and caressing my back while we inhaled each other's scents when he let me go, he smirked at me pouting.

I know I had a sad look on my face because I didn't want him to leave. I thoroughly enjoyed Midas company. His touch, his laid-back persona. Everything that came out of his mouth was meaningful. What really turned me on was that he was about his business, very respectful, he didn't come over here on some horny wanting to fuck me and leave me. He had good self-control and wasn't out here slanging dick to every good-looking woman he saw just because he had money. He really came over to get to know me and dig as deep as I allowed him to. I couldn't wait to see him tomorrow when I got to the hospital, I even thought about bringing him lunch.

I sat in my bed thinking about Midas, I told myself not to move too fast with him. He had an edge to him that was dangerous, but it was intriguing at the same time. The part that I liked the most about our conversation was him realizing the things that needed correction within himself. That was a sign of a man who was willing to take accountability. Which was hard to find in men today. Midas was also open to making changes in his life. One thing for sure was that he had the Midas touch. His touch was tantalizing, I opened my nightstand and pulled out my Rose toy. Laying back, I opened my legs and thought of Midas as the Rose did its job.

NAYVIUS

 ne week later

"I'M SICK AS FUCK MAN." I shook my head. My outburst got the attention of Midas and Shooter. We sat in Midas backyard smoking a celebration blunt. Ms. Wellington woke up and was alert and talking a little. She still had a long road to recovery but that was good enough for us. The first thing she told Midas was go home and rest. Midas didn't listen, instead, he had me, and Shooter meet him here to smoke outside and prepare to ride out to end Histori's life.

"I'm having trouble breathing, my hands be randomly shaking and shit. Feels like I'm having withdrawals from some shit. I even get the chills like I'm cold." I frowned up, not liking the new symptoms that I had been experiencing.

"Nigga, need to go to the doctor. Midas, put that blunt out. We ain't smoking behind this nigga." Shooter stared at me accusingly. Midas chuckled and kept taking long drags from the blunt.

"That goofy ass nigga ain't sick. He really too old to be acting the way that he acts." I started to cough and clutch my chest like I was experiencing the worse pain. These niggas never took me fucking serious. I was really sick as hell and hated that I felt this way.

"Go after what it is you want nigga but smoothly do that shit. You out here looking like a loss fucking dog, starving. Return back to owner." Midas grumbled. He was in killer mode right now. His persona always turned dark when it was time for us to go handle some shit.

"I don't got no owner, and Shooter I don't need no fuckin doctor. I need..." I fake coughed, swallowing down my spit and making a sour face.

"I need Jaiden. I don't know why she doing this weird ass shit and I don't know why I'm even feigning for her like this. This shit is crazy my niggas. Jaiden got me fucked up in a real way if she thinks she gone just cut me off for months with the kind of..." I stopped talking. Jaiden's pussy was so good that I didn't even want to brag about the shit. These were my niggas, and I knew that they probably would never try to play me.

I just didn't want niggas seeing Jaiden and imagining what was between her legs. Niggas always could brag about how good a hoe pussy was. Jaiden was a woman a real one at that, and I was actually trying to see what all we could be. I respected her not to even call her out of her name and brag on how good she was in bed.

I looked up and saw Shooter and Midas cracking the fuck up. Usually, I'd join them laughing but I couldn't. I really missed Jaiden down to the talking we did on the phone. She made me want to do shit differently. I didn't want to be an alcoholic drinking my life away to take the pain away like I normally did from the loss of my parents.

Jaiden came into my life and took that pain away with just being herself. Everything she did made me admire her. The way she took care of business and chased after her dreams. She always talked about her kids and when she talked about them her eyes lit up like they were her entire world. She didn't have much and wasn't laced in designer, but she kept herself clean including her apartment. In my opinion women didn't need designers to look beautiful. It was the confidence and the owner inside the clothes that made the outfit pop out more.

"You let her cut you off nigga." Midas chuckled, placing the blunt inside of the ashtray. I touched my chin like I was taking the time to think.

"You right, I did warn her and tell her what type of nigga I would be if she did this dumb shit. She thinks this shit with me is Disney, when I'm on some Rated R type of timing. Bet." Was all I said in conclusion. It was time for me to apply the right amount of pressure to show Jaiden that she was stuck with me. Shooter snickered and stood up to his feet.

"Rated R huh? Nigga you don't know shit about a relationship. You already fucked it up before the shit could even get started. Sounds like Vanessa was more of your league and fucking bitches, making money and keep it pushing. It's the best for niggas like us. We got the money for the lifestyle."

"We getting older though. Besides that, we too old for all of that. If you find a woman you can vibe with why not try to build on that. Do you see the kind of generation that we are surrounded by. The mind frames and how these youngin's think? I ain't tryna stick my dick in different bitches and have them using me and plotting on ways to secure the bag." Me and Shooter both looked at Midas and raised our brows.

"The fuck wrong with you? You sure you ain't sick like

this nigga Goof?" Shooter pestered around; I tittered a little because this shit was amusing as fuck to see Midas talking this way. He swore on everything that he loved after Zori and Princess how he would never open up to being with another chick.

"Who is she?" I asked, already knowing who it was.

"Aww hell naw nigga! You will not be my father-in-law! You need to pick somebody else!" Midas laughed but I was serious as hell.

"I like her a lot, I see it turning into love the more I talk to her. She different."

"She different." Shooter mocked Midas.

"Look how you looking, you already in love nigga. Damn y'all just leaving all the hoes for me. I'm good with that. I love this generation of new bitches. Keep a nigga fit and on my toes." Midas shook his head then looked off at nothing in particular as he spoke.

"On some real shit my niggas… besides all the funny shit. I been thinking over a lot of shit lately. I see change and growth… it can be for the better of all of us. I talked with my son Logic and after I teach him the ropes of the drug side and everything about the college for when I'm ready to retire. I really want the nigga to give up being a Kingpin but it's what he chooses to be. The school shit, I'm doing that until I'm ready to give up and pass that down as well. Drug wise I see myself washing my hands once I feel Logic has it down pack."

I nodded my head in agreement while looking up at Shooter. Something passed through his eyes, and I tried to ignore it but couldn't. I had this gnawing feeling inside of me that told me shit was going to go left. Fire blazed and danced around in his eyes. He chewed on his bottom lip like he was fighting back speaking his mind. I knew Shooter well enough to know that he wouldn't hold back. He would surely say what he was thinking.

"That's really foul my nigga. You don't even know that lil nigga and you gone put him before me and Goof!" His voice was loud as hell now. I sat back in my chair watching everyone's movement.

"Don't put me in that my nigga. I'm good with where I'm at. I've already been making moves to ensure that my money will always flow." That was the truth. I never wanted to take over any Midas shit. I had my own shit in motion. I invested in so much property that I needed more time on my hands to take care of my own business.

The first thing that I needed to work on was my temper. Legal business wasn't like the drug game. You couldn't just get mad at people, pull out your gun like Midas was doing right now and end a person's life.

"That's my son." Midas jaw clenched.

"And? Nigga you always been on some weird shit, and I shouldn't of let shit slide from jump with you killing Darius."

"So, what you saying nigga? You thought you was coming in to save the day when my momma got hit? You thought that shit would solidify you a spot in my shoes?"

"Nigga fuck you!" Shooter pulled his gun and by the time I reached for mine, Midas had already shot him in the head. I watched his body drop as Midas tilted his head, as if he was listening to music.

"A minute to pray…"

"A second to die…" I completed his sentence as Midas stood up and nodded his head at me.

"They smiling in ya face, all the time they want to take your place. The backstabbers." Midas sung lowly.

"Backstabbers!" I sang the ad libs as we walked out of the backyard. I couldn't hold back the laugh if I wanted to and surprisingly Midas joined in and laughed too.

"Nigga had to go."

"He did, and that ain't shit you got to explain to me." I closed the sliding door behind me.

"One of the men told me that he took ten racks from Shooter. Shooter was going to set Histori free. I guess Shooter was trying to find the courage to shoot me." Midas chuckled dryly; I could tell that the shit was fucking with him.

We walked through the house as Midas texted on his burner phone. I already knew he was getting the cleanup crew here to make Shooter disappear out of his backyard.

"Shit kind of fuck with me because I got love for that nigga. It sucks he couldn't live to see another day." I fake sniffled and wiped my dry face.

"Too bad, so sad." I sniffled again and fell out laughing all over again.

"And there were two men." Midas opened his front door as I followed behind him, shutting the door.

"Two men that's about to go kill this bitch ass nigga and work towards change." I added.

"My nigga." We slapped hands and headed to the warehouse. After all of this was done. I was going to put a plan together to go see about Jaiden. I knew that she was pissed how I got up in the middle of us fucking to leave. I just couldn't explain to her why I had to do what I had to do. That was a part of my life that I didn't want her involved in.

"Through understanding people will grow. We both understand that in order to grow we have to be understanding to change. When I saw my momma… all of that blood was too much for me. You see it made me pass out. When I woke up shit was still the same but a little worse. She was in a coma then they took half of her brain out. Shit had me so fucked up, I thought about all the conversations that me and my momma had. It also made me understand clearer on how you feel my nigga. Why you drink and try to block out the pain from not having both parents here. Shit is something vicious, but it made me want to understand the changes that life brings on. Time never stops but other things do, like the breaths we take every second. We make so much money, we invest, we avoid getting caught up… so what do we do from here? Keep avoiding, or live better and do better. I can let the drug shit completely go and don't pass shit down to Logic. What you think he will do? Find another way, so I give it to him but with guidance. I'll explain to him the understanding that he needs to have when it comes to this shit. Eventually, I pray he leaves it alone and grow as a man like I'm doing now."

Midas had a look of worry in his eyes. I could only imagine how he felt. Knowing he had a grown son who was already a kingpin and set on wanting to continue being one. The good thing about Logic was that he was smart. He had already invested and had legal money coming in. Midas technically had no say so in what Logic wanted to do but I knew Midas very well. Midas had a way with words and getting through to people.

"Well, you know that I'm locked in with you for life. I kind of feel like if I get serious with Jaiden, I gotta keep my nose clean. I wouldn't be able to take it if something happen to her or her kids because of me. She gives me peace; I want to be the same thing for her. I don't want her worried about me and what I don't tell her and I damn sure don't want her thinking that I'm keeping shit from her. I really like her my nigga and I'm starting to think that the shit is love."

"Yea I feel you; I'm starting to feel the same way about her momma." Midas looked over at me and smirked with his dumb ass.

MIDAS

"$\mathcal{I}$t's a good day to die today." I looked up at the gloomy sky. Wintertime in California was always bipolar. It could either be sunny or cloudy with a cool breeze. My mom used to get so excited when she saw clouds in the sky, hoping that it would rain. It hardly ever rained in Southern California, whenever it did people were pissed but I embraced it.

It started to drizzle slowly as I looked up to the sky. Happy that my mom's hospital room had big windows inside so she could enjoy the view. I snapped out of the thoughts of my mother and thought about my father. What I was about to do, he would've done himself without thinking twice about Histori being his son. Hell, if I was Histori, my father would kill me.

My father was a firm believer in his wife coming first before anybody. He always said that it was supposed to be that way even when I had kids of my own. Kids watch their parents and see how the love flows between the two. When they get older, they go make families of their own and love the way that they were taught.

I learned from my father's mistakes and when I made mistakes of my own, I stood on them like a man is supposed to. A lot of things weren't mistakes like people liked to say. It was bad decision making, wondering what the outcome would be. When my father cheated on my mother, it was a poor decision that he had made. He admitted to it and went through the consequences never disrespecting my mother in the process. That was the first time I witnessed seeing fear in my father's eyes. It was the first time that I saw him bothered and hurt. He said how it hurt him even more to see my mother so distraught and it tore him apart being away like my mother requested so she could think it through and weigh it out.

Histori was a decision between my father and his side chick. A decision that was given a fair chance and an equal amount of love. I could've killed him when I found out he set me up and stole from me, no I should've killed him like Shooter said. Histori wanted me dead but wasn't man enough to face me and handle the job by himself. He sent some gutter rat bitches to take me out and even they couldn't complete the job. I could have even killed him when I brought him to the table and gave him a fair opportunity to make money and he took that and flipped it by stealing. I kept him alive because I understood the poor decisions he made; they weren't mistakes he did the shit by choice.

Shit that I killed less for; I kept him alive a little longer because he was a part of my father. I should have realized that my mother was a piece of my father and so was I. We were the best parts of him left and now my son was. He was inside this warehouse that I stood on the outside of. I needed to see if he even had it in him to do what it was that I was about to do.

Killing came easy to me, I conditioned my conscience for

it. It was easy, you could be here today and gone tomorrow. I was somebody's unforeseen occurrence waiting to happen if you fucked with me in the wrong way. This was the change that I was talking about. I wanted to feel more, be aware of things being done the right way. I needed to get the demon that was planted inside of my soul out. Get the rage and anger that fueled my inner demon out.

I flicked the blunt that was burning between my index and thumb away from me and took my surroundings in one last time. This warehouse was in foreclosure when I first purchased it. I placed an office inside on the second level, while the first level had boxes of different shipments to make it appear like it was operating strictly for business. I had access to so many things that a lot of properties went to waste while some were put to good use.

No one came here or knew about this place except the people who needed to. When I got to the double doors, my phone started to ring. My entire mood shifted when I saw that it was Aubry calling.

"Aubry." I smiled, releasing the door handle. I gave the double doors my back as I leaned up against the frame.

"I just love how you say my name Midas." I loved the way she said my name and how her voice was soft it held no aggression in it. Aubry's voice sounded seductive and melodic, she could be saying regular shit and it made me brick up.

"I was calling to tell you that Ms. Wellington has made more progress. She knows her name and what year it is. She even asked for you, I'm waiting on the speech therapist to come in because she still is talking with a bit of a slur. She sucked through a straw and ate a little bit of applesauce. She seems to get tired quickly if she have to put in too much work with chewing. I did let the nurses know not to let her continue sucking through straws because she still has a sinus drainage. Also, we will keep her on soft foods for a couple of days so when you come up here, eat first. I don't want her smelling outside food then wanting it." I could hear it in her voice that she was smiling. I was smiling as well because it felt good to have someone taking care of my mom that actually loved her job.

I told Aubry that I wanted good news first then bad news last when it came to my mom. I was still stressed out, hoping nothing went wrong. Aubry and my mom's other doctors thought it was a big miracle how my mom was moving fast towards recovery especially considering her age. I was worried about when it came time for them to do another head surgery placing the right side of her brain and bone back in to fix the structure of her head.

Right now, that side of her head was caved in because the bone was missing. One side of her face looked like her, but the other side had to be reconstructed which Aubry stated that it would go back to normal. They just didn't know if my mother's right eye would open back up.

"Thanks baby, and the bad news?" my stomach turned a little as I braced myself.

"Bad news is she has aspiration pneumonia in the back of her lungs that is causing her high fevers. We are treating that with antibiotics. Remember I told you when the brain is injured, other parts of the body start getting minor to severe infections. Tonight, the neuro doctor wants to have another test done to check the vessels in her brain. Overall, she is in good spirits and it's nothing too major to worry about." I released the breath that I was holding and lightened my grip from the phone.

"Good, I really appreciate you." I sighed, rubbing the back of my neck.

"Hey? One day at a time. Praying to God and staying positive as well as patience will get us all through this." *Us?* That is what I really liked about Aubry she was selfless. I appreciated this woman so much.

"You right, I'm working on the patience part when it comes to her. I know that I have to have that in order to support her thoroughly. Other than that, how is your day going?"

"It's going good, I plan on going to see my daughter once I get off work from here. Hopefully you make it up here so I can see you." Her voice dropped lower.

"I can make that happen, I'm wrapping up business and I plan to be on my way up there to stay the night."

"Sounds like you up to no good." My brows instinctively rose as I released a chuckle.

"How it sound like that?" She was very observant, like most women were. Always trying to investigate and follow their intuition.

"When I talk to you, I never hear wind blowing like I do now. So, you're outside somewhere waiting to go in. You're keeping your sentences short with me as well as the flirting that you normally do. It's okay, I understand but I do want to talk about it more later when you're free." Aubry sounded hopeful but this wasn't something I would probably ever tell her.

"Member the change that I mentioned to you." She remained silent.

"This is a part of the change that I was talking about when I came to your house. After this, I hope I never have to revert to this old way of doing things Aubry. I know you're a smart woman and can read in between the lines of what I'm trying to say. What I'm up to now is not up for discussion and we won't talk about it ever. I want you, and I want you to have a different version of me. Not this version right now."

"I can understand it."

"That's all I need is understanding. I don't want to come to you, and you try to fight the demons that I need to fight on my own. I want to come to you fully Aubry. Not with trust issues or past issues. I don't even want to live a double life hiding things for your protection. Something inside of me, tells me that you're the woman that was crafted and sent straight from God as a sign of forgiveness. If I do things wrong with you, then I'll mess up that second chance from God." I didn't have any other words for Aubry right now because I felt myself getting into emotions.

Right now, I need a dead conscious and for me not to feel anything. When I walked out of this warehouse. I was headed to see my mom, to confide and tell her all about this side of me. She would understand it better than anyone. I would repent and promise God that I would no longer move this way and kill just because someone had wronged me. The next time or if I did have to kill again, it would be for me or my family protection.

I grew so accustomed to this shit that I was immune and heartless when it came to this side of things. In order for me to feel deep love, like the love I pictured from Aubry, I had to release these killer demons inside of me. When I hung the phone up, I stood up straight off the warehouse door then turned to face the door trying my hardest to rid myself of the emotions lodged inside of me when talking to Aubry and thinking about my mother's healing journey.

My mom might not ever be the same and for that alone Histori had to pay. My mind went back to a conversation me and my mom had and I dropped my head. She was right all along but she was wrong about Histori.

"You gotta live right one day son, killing people for control doesn't make things right. I can't keep praying for you when you not even helping yourself." My mood soured. I stiffened and now I was no longer in the mood to sit here and get my hair re-coiled.

"It's my way of life. Not yours, I don't force it on you. Just like I don't force you to pray for me." Whap! The back of my neck stung, I shut my eyes and listened to the sound of the vacuum cleaner start up.

"Nigga don't come in my house with ya tight ass suit, disrespecting me in my shit. Better take your stuck up ass around the corner and get one of them stylist to do your shit. Hell, my fingers hurt any damn way." Before she could issue another hit to the back of my neck, I stood up.

Buttoning up my suit, I went to take a seat on the loveseat across from her small sectional couch. She reached for her pack of cigarettes and pulled one out to light it. Goof finished vacuuming and didn't need to be told to leave.

He pecked my mom on the forehead, nodded his head at me, and left out.

"Do I ever tell you about yourself?" I asked my mom calmly. I didn't want her to get herself worked up like she normally did whenever she felt like someone was challenging her. I was thirty-eight years old, and I still gave my mom the respect she deserved. I didn't curse, drink or smoke around her. I sure as hell didn't impose my lifestyle onto her either but she knew exactly what I was about.

She wasn't dumb, she fell in love with my father, and he was way worse than I. My grandfather and grandmother lived the same way that I was living and passed the torch to my father and uncles who taught me the shit.

Things were wrapped so tight and well that nothing could possibly go wrong. Even things being damn near perfect, I never slacked, and I never bullshitted around. I lived a basic ass lifestyle never bringing attention to myself. I wasn't a flashy nigga; I didn't have a million cars and mega mansions like I could have had.

If any fed that wasn't in my back pocket looked me up and tried to investigate me, they would see me as the Chancellor of the University of So-Cal College. It was a successful black college run by a board of trustees. All the trustees were a part of my family. As far as it being run by the state it was a no-go. We made it private before my father died. I became the founder and was working like hell to get another one opened in Vegas.

The state was all a part of the big drug trade back in the sixties, so they turned a blind eye to how it was built and how the money got put into UOSC. We didn't use public dollars to finance it. Public dollars came years later. Now, I no longer had to put funds into the college because funds were generated through a variety of sources. Research grants, tuition, donations, athletics, and in-state government support. I had the government in my other back pocket as well with the drug harvest giving them a percentage that kept the laws off my fucking back.

I had people in place at the college to maintain laboratories, structures, libraries, and computer resources, which was very expensive. I wasn't lazy at all; I was hands-on with my drug crops as well as the college. I made sure the faculty and staff were thorough and had proper qualifications. With that, they were paid and credited. Everything cost and millions were spent on in-home security and dorms. The list went on and on.

My mother knew about all of this, I didn't leave her in the dark because if shit was to turn left, I didn't want to leave her to pick up the pieces. If I ever got exposed, which the chances were slim to none, I made it to where I wouldn't lose the college. It would look as if I got involved with someone who forced me to do it. A person was in place for that as well.

I had several degrees, I moved shit like I was playing a lifetime game of chess. I barely rested at night because I was too busy thinking. My thoughts never stopped, and I understood why. I had a lot riding on my back and shoulders.

"Midas, your filthy rich baby. The drugs, and pointless killing all because of your ego needs to stop." She eyed me sternly.

"The drugs are what built this ma. It pays the bills for thousands. Black boys and girls get a good education and leave college to live the American dream." She didn't understand that there was no backing away. I wasn't some corner hustler. I was a distributor, not just for kingpins but for people that called the fucking shots and made shit tick then tock.

The government was one of my biggest customers. I never let my mom in on that. She viewed me as the average kingpin. She wouldn't even understand how surgeons used cocaine in sinus surgery and in plenty of other surgeries they used the shit. Operative pain control, they needed cocaine and heroin. They used heroin in a lot of shit as well. They mixed it down in a lot of opioids. Marijuana had its uses too.

All my shit was pure and did its job. Besides kingpins using the shit to sell and make lots of money. I was putting the shit to good use and the government knew nothing about my illegal side in all of this.

"All I'm saying son, is that college brings in lots of money. You're getting older, it's time you had kids and settle down with a nice woman. I want grandkids, Midas. Gail doesn't have any kids so it would be nice to have little babies running around. We all getting old, me, you, your aunt."

"Maybe you should look into adopting Ma. Love isn't in the cards for me."

"It could be in the cards for you if you let it. Princess was a good girl; Lord knows what you did to her." I fake stretched and stood up. It felt like my mom had kicked me right in the balls. She was in one of her moods today. A lot must have been worrying her. She was skipping around topics and speaking on shit that I didn't want to hear about.

"Lord knows what she did to me." I mumbled and looked at my mom with conflicted eyes. She got me in my feelings that fast and that didn't happen often. Parents had a way of pushing all of your buttons. My mom was good at doing that.

"I gotta go ma." Fuck my hair, I'd wash it and go to the salon and let someone twist it up for me.

"Your brother Histori called me yesterday." That stopped me from walking out. I took a seat and cracked my neck from side to side, wondering just what his bitch ass wanted. I kept my distance for several reasons. I was a man with lots of understanding, even as a kid I always had some form of understanding.

I remember when my father crushed my mom by being upfront telling her he had another son that was a little younger than me. He didn't say it was a slip up or something he didn't want to do like most niggas would have said. He was upfront and told her with no shame or hesitation that he had a son who he named Histori.

My mom broke down right in front of him, she cried like he had told her that someone had died. My father got down on the kitchen floor and held my mother. Until her cries got low and she asked him why? She told him that he should have kept that to himself instead of hurting her. He explained how he wanted both of his sons to be close and for us to know each other.

99

Later that night, my father came into my room and instead of explaining the situation he told me straight up. "When a man fucks up, he owns up to it. Don't matter who you hurt Midas or who you love, you keep shit real with the people you love. I'll never leave your momma, but I also told her from the beginning that I will always have multiple women that will never come before her. She accepted that, and we moved forward in life. Did I mean to have a kid in the process, no. I never wanted a broken family. For years I didn't believe it or even acknowledge the lil nigga until his momma finally got the DNA test that I had been asking her to take. The proof is in, and today I had to tell your mom the real. She might be sad for a while, so don't be around here making shit harder on her. You understand that?"

I understood it well, I always try to make shit less complicated. I'm the nigga that understands that everyone is not like me. People don't have the same capabilities and mind frame that I have, and I don't fault them for that shit. When a person crosses me, then the understanding stops. I either cut you off or kill you. Since my father wanted me to love and be there for Histori. I decided to cut his punk ass off the first time his dumb ass stole from me.

I overlooked a lot of shit with Histori, I overlooked the jealousy and envy that was evident in his eyes every time he came around. I gave him a seat at my table and fed him in ways that I didn't have to. He let his greed ruin whatever relationship we had as brothers. Nigga was taking cocaine and weed to sell for his own benefit when he didn't even put the work in to try to have the audacity to take from me.

I did what was best and that was me beating his ass and letting him know that his best bet would be to stay the fuck away from me. He was fucking with me now, calling my mom, a woman who never even liked your mom to begin with, was like calling me. He had to know that my mom would tell me because I'm her son.

"His mom passed away. He told me that he had been expecting it she was in her last stage with cancer."

"My condolences, you tell him I said that and let him know about the deal we made." I pulled my phone out of the inside of my suit jacket and silenced it. Shooter was calling, I'd made a mental note to call him back.

"The deal about him staying away or else you would kill him? Midas, fuck that deal. This is your brother, and you need to be there for him. We are going to his mother's funeral." She shook her head as I offered a crooked smile.

"So be it, mother."

"Don't you start that sarcastic shit with me, Midas." I let out a chuckle and nodded my head standing to my feet.

"No sarcasm mam, if you insist that I go, then I will be there. Let me know what color dress you wearing so my tie can match." I stood up and went to give her a kiss on each chubby cheek. I usually would stay longer, but right now, I was itching to smoke a blunt and plan my approach at Histori's mother's funeral.

My mom wanted me to go, I could opt out but now I was curious. Maybe he needed to see my face as a reminder of how I give it up when I say that I'm done with a person. I really hated when muthafuckas made me regret not killing them.

MIDAS

*H*istori sat in an old wooden chair that was barely holding him up by the legs. His eyes were swollen, lips cracked. His naked body was battered badly. I looked over at Diamond, he studied him intently. I didn't know what the exact reason fire was being displayed in my son's eyes, but it was enough to tell me that he was built and ready for whatever it was that was about to take place.

Goof held a rusted metal chain; he swung it lowly back and forth making sure it scraped the ground each time he moved it.

"My mom is up and doing well, can you believe that shit? She survived your punk ass attempt on her life my nigga." I smirked at Histori. He struggled with keeping his head up to focus on who was talking to him. When he realized that it was me, he made a squealing noise. It's been months since Histori saw me, I kept his ass in here with only Goof and Shooter and the men that were paid to stand on guard watching him.

He took three ass beatings daily and was given enough nutrition to give him the energy and feeling to register what was happening to him. I wanted him to live in hell every day of my mom being in a coma until she woke up before I put him out of his misery. Grabbing a folding chair, I dragged it until it was in front of Histori. Taking a seat, I placed my index finger on his bloody forehead until his eyes were locked in on mine.

"I'm a very understanding man, Histori. I wanted to keep your shiesty ass alive because we share the same blood. I just can't and won't try to understand all of your betrayal. I won't even try to understand how you could hurt one of the sweetest woman that would have literally accepted you as her son since your mother is dead." I shook my head at his stupid ass, watching the tears well up in his eyes were pointless.

"Thank God my mother survived because if she didn't Histori. I would keep you alive every day and make you feel like you were dying and dead."

"I-I-I…." Each letter he spoke he choked and coughed and frowned his face up like it was painful. He had splits and bloody cuts along his top and bottom lip like one of the men cut him with razors.

"I-I-I'm so-sorry." He looked relieved to get that out as he let out a low whimper. His crying was an attempt to beg for the life he tried to wrong people for. I pulled my gun and nodded my head in final understanding.

"Yea me too brother." Pulling him by his shoulder, I brought him close like I was trying to render over a hug to him. He yelped out and squirmed from being in so much pain. When he was close enough, I placed my gun underneath his chin and blew his brain out. I was in a zone and what brought me out of that zone was the sound of my gun clicking letting me know that I emptied the clip in him.

Releasing his body, he fell sideways. I sat there looking at him for a couple of seconds until I no longer wanted to see him. Standing up, the first person I made eye contact with was Diamond.

"That was gangsta as fuck." Diamond smiled brightly like he was pumped up. Goof dropped the chain and started to laugh. He laughed and clutched his stomach like it hurt.

"Oh, this lil nigga really with the shits. I'm gone enjoy training him." Diamond frowned his face up and looked at me in confusion. I nodded my head at Diamond as Goof walked away with his burner phone glued to his ear. I already knew he was on the line with the cleanup crew. I took this time to take Diamond up to my office to have a talk with him.

We got to the second floor, and I immediately went into the bathroom that was attached to my office area and cleaned off all the blood that was splattered all over my face and neck. I was back to my normal self and had already forgotten all about Histori.

When I walked back into my office area, Diamond was on the phone with Princess on speaker. I listened to them converse then tuned out their conversation. I rolled up a blunt and took a couple of hits. Soon as Diamond was off the phone I started talking.

"How long do you see yourself being a Kingpin and businessman?" This was the second time I asked him this, I was hoping that his answer would be the one that I wanted to hear but at the same time, Diamond was young. When I was his age, it was the power and all the money that was coming in from what I was doing that had me stuck.

"Until I'm about forty. Maybe even younger if I get tired of the street shit. I eat, breathe, and sleep to it. I didn't grow up having it all, shit my foster momma was a functional dope fiend she taught me more than she thinks when it comes to this survival shit." He shrugged, pulling out a cigarette.

"You no longer have to be on survival shit. You got me

now, and I can set you up good financially to where you can invest in other shit so you can turn and walk away from the street shit. I hate that you are a part of me and came from me and even had to see the struggle because I never saw it."

"Then you won't understand me not wanting to leave. I know this is on some wanting better for me because I'm your son and you missed out on time. You can't fault yourself for that shit when you didn't have a choice and decision in it. What happened, happened and I'm a grown man now, I made something out of nothing and have my own life that I've been living to the best of my ability."

"I respect that, I don't want to step on your toes, but I want to continue to get to know you and be here for you from here on out. I trust you and that's new for me, but it came natural because you are my son. I can see so much of me, and your grandfather lodged into you. I also see you bumping your head along the way but at least I'm here now to help you as much as I can." He nodded his head and looked away like he was thinking about what I was saying.

"What is that nigga Goof talking about when he says train me?"

"He mean exactly what he say. Train you. Something him and I will do if you're willing to learn." I hit my blunt one more time before putting it out and sitting up in my seat to have this talk with Diamond.

"I'm ready for change, with this change I can walk away from being the plug or I can pass it down to you. I can't just give it to you without teaching and preparing you for it. It's not just some turf or you slanging bricks. It's bigger than that, millions of dollars being made every time you plop down on the toilet to take a shit. You have to fall in love with staying on top of things and keeping the ones that work for you in line. You will be overseeing the proper growth of your drugs. You will have sit-down talks with people that's not a part of the streets but love what the streets provide. Hospitals need pure product to use for different things when it comes to patients. Big money, government money that will keep you from taking a trip to jail. I'm offering you connections that you will never see if you were to remain a local Kingpin."

I sat back into my seat and waited for Diamond's response. He looked like he was stunned trying to process everything that I just said.

"You ready to walk away from that?" I nodded my head first, before I answered.

"I'm ready to walk away now if I could but I have to train you first and Goof will assist with that. You have to be ready to walk away at a certain point as well. I think that is the biggest mistake that your grandfather made. I almost made the same mistake as him. Your grandfather stayed in it so long that it threw off his proper judgment in some things. If I give you this, the college will eventually come with every-thing. I will help you on both ends but I'm not giving up college just yet. I still need something to do, and I actually enjoy being up at the college…Oh and you have to dress the part, look like a businessman. All that sagging showing ya ass and wearing all the loud jewelry needs to tone down. Just because you become wealthy and have tons of money doesn't mean the entire world needs to know. Don't bring too much attention to yourself." I smiled because by the looks of it, Diamond dressed and flaunted his shit in a way that would make a broke nigga tempted to rob him. He was a walking lick, an easy come up. On his neck, wrist, and fingers, I counted a smooth million. The clothes that he had on his back and ass was somebody in high ass Cali rent or mortgage payment.

"I'm with it, a nigga nervous because this some big ass shit. Like I never imagine being a part of some shit like this."

"You and Princess... what's going on with that." I changed the topic because I didn't want my son blinded by her.

"I got love for her. I mean I'm young as fuck, but I like her a lot. At first, I wanted to turn my back on her especially given the circumstances, but she needs someone solid in her corner even if I just be a friend to her." I liked his response.

"A woman can make a man do wild things. A woman that's really the one for you will have you changing your ways and making you become a better man. She'll be down for you but eventually she will see the bigger picture and tell you that she wants more for you. Meaning she will eventually want you to get out of the lifestyle that you're living because she's tired of stressing from the long nights of you being away from her. I'm talking to a woman now that I feel like if I was too open up and tell her everything. She wouldn't want that for me. I mean she might accept my way of living for a little bit but then it'll become a burden, and she will eventually start to press me for change. I like this woman so much that I'm willing to make that change. Plus, I'm at a stage in my life where I just want more peace. I want to come home and do all the shit regular people do. So, I say that to say, don't put your eggs in one basket especially if your still into playing the field."

I picked up my half of blunt and re sparked it. It felt good to have this face-to-face talk with Diamond. We talked on the phone here and there, but this right here was better.

"Princess is a work in progress. I truly believe besides how she did me and beyond that bitch ass nigga that I just killed and her fucked up ass momma.... I believe she has a good heart and means well. She just has to find herself. Make herself happy first before she can make someone else happy. She's broken and need the pieces to her puzzle put back together. Either you help her fix those pieces and make it clear to her what your intentions with her is. Doesn't matter if its friends with benefits, a relationship or just fuck buddies. Princess is a different breed who is already moving off of how bad she's been hurt throughout life. She uses that as an excuse for the way that she moves. She also has taken enough blows and hits, it's a big part of the reason why she is the woman that she is today. I don't know who that woman is like that now because what we had was real to me but something else for her. Her heart was with that nigga that just died today. You know the Princess she is now so that's what you go by, what she has shown you son."

"I know... I wonder if I really want to fuck with her and try to be on some real shit with her. How would I even determine if she sincere and really fuck with me the same." I shrugged my shoulders as I thought about it.

"Sometimes it's hard to tell if a person really rocks with you. I just killed one of my boys that I never thought I would have to kill. I killed my brother today and for years I tried to respect and uphold my father wishes. Situations and people change all the time, but money never changes. Make sure if she changes that she don't cause your money to change too. You get my drift, don't you?"

"That's a hunnid right there."

"It is, so whatever you do decide to do with her... make sure you always make yourself clear." I looked at my watch and my mom and Aubry face flashed in my head. I continued to talk with Diamond until Goof came upstairs to tell me that everything was handled. Smoking another blunt with Diamond and Goof we came up with a schedule to meet with Diamond throughout the week to start him with training.

* * *

I MADE it to the hospital about two hours after I left the warehouse. I couldn't come straight here without going home first to shower and rid myself of remnants of Histori. I checked in at the front desk and got my visitor badge and headed up to the sixth floor ICU. I couldn't wait until my mom was able to get off of this floor and go to another because ICU constantly had traffic. Something was always happening that had nurses everywhere like flies on shit.

I didn't get good rest because they checked in on my mom every twenty minutes to make sure she was good. I didn't complain or appear frustrated because I wanted her to receive all the proper care that she could get. When they gave the okay for her to go to another room, I planned to hire a team so she could finish healing from home. I wanted her as comfortable as possible.

The first person I saw was Aubry. She stood at the nurse station with a clip board in her hand. I stood next to the elevator observing her intently. She yawned as she was in the middle of talking to a group of nurses. Rubbing her eyes, she ran her fingers through her hair and smiled. Her side view was perfect, even with her white, long doctor jacket, the curves on her couldn't be missed.

I loved when women wore their real hair down with no extensions just pressed and laid to perfection in its natural state. Aubry had thick ass silky straight hair. Her presence could be felt from a distance. I could just imagine how good she smelled and how hard it would be for me to resist wanting to pull her into my arms and hold her close up against my body and just inhale her.

Aubry felt like home, I was infatuated with all of her. She was like that closed book that you wanted to open up and read over and over. She would be my favorite story that I would always enjoy. I wanted to speed shit up every time I laid eyes on her, I just understood that with her she was like fine China. You had to tread carefully. I didn't want to mess things up and I already knew that I had to step shit up.

She yawned again and turned a little in my direction. Like a magnet our eyes locked into one another, and she fought her smile until she gave in. Her deep dimples sunk into her chubby cheeks, and she blushed hard my way. She excused herself and started towards me with her clip board leading the way. Aubry was inches away when her sexy scent drifted up my nose. Tucking my hands in my pockets to keep from grabbing her by the waist and pulling her close, she stopped in front of me, smile never wavering.

"It's good to see you Mr. Wellington, my office is on the next floor. Take the elevators up with me so I can give you something that I know you didn't take the time to get before you go see Ms. Wellington." My stomach grumbled as she walked in front of me. I picked up my feet and anxiously followed behind her. I loved Aubry's cooking. I admired the fact that she could actually throw down and preferred to eat home-cooked food instead of constantly buying out.

I hated fast food, home-cooked meals had more meaning and flavor to it. She held her office door open for me, and I stepped in and listened to her shut the door.

"So, I cooked beef stew with potatoes, carrots and different veggies are-," I turned and delicately grabbed her around her waist and pulled her in close for a tight hug. My touch made her inhale sharply, then expel her breath in a slow, steady hiss. I bent down to meet her short frame and kissed her on the neck, moving her silky thick hair to the side, I took a long sniff.

"Damn you always smell so fucking good baby." She put

her arms around my neck then massaged the back of my neck, her soft fingers went to my shoulder blades and worked her magic. Aubry had me closing my eyes enjoying the feeling of her working out all the tension that I had pent up. I have never received a massage a day in my life. She had me ready to get on my knees and propose with the way she worked her hands.

"I'm so happy to see you, I wish that we could spend more time together. I hope that doesn't sound like I'm trying to be clingy." Her voice held need and skepticism.

"You sound like a grown woman that knows what she wants. Always speak your mind with me. I want to spend more time with you too. I want to properly date you as well. Open you up more to me because I'm ready to open up to you. I know exactly what and who I want Aubry... that's you, all of you. So, I'm not going to half step. I'm going to do this shit right." I indicated, staring her deeply in the eyes.

Moving her jacket, I went underneath her shirt and touched her back. Rubbing it slowly to give her comfort, my fingers tingled as they skimmed over her soft ass skin. I slid my hands down the back of her scrubs, gripping her ass, I squeezed tight then rubbed up and down. Placing my forehead against hers, I just stared into her eyes as she relaxed against me.

"I want you real bad. I'm drawn to you, you're beautiful, smart, and caring..." Her fingers threaded through my hair; I closed my eyes appreciating her touch.

"You make me want to speed shit up with you Aubry. I just don't want to scare you." My fingers now danced over her stomach then skimmed down until my hand was inside of her scrubs. Somehow this was turning sexual, I was in need and the way she was holding her breath and moaning lowly while her hands were now touching my hair, neck, and ears. I used my free hand to go under her bra, teasing her right nipple making it grow hard.

Moving her panties to the side, my fingers had a mind of their own. Her mound was fat, when they traveled to her thick pussy lips, wetness soaked my fingertips. My dick was twitching, and I started thinking about getting down on her office floor, throwing her leg over my shoulder and eating her pussy until she was screaming my name. I couldn't do that, and I couldn't have her in this way. I needed space, a bed, and much more to do all I needed to do to Aubry. Once I got inside of her there would be no stopping or sliding out of her anytime soon, so this was indeed the wrong place and time to be getting this aroused.

"I want to feel you Midas." She didn't want, she needed to feel me inside of her. I knew it because I needed to feel her. I pushed two fingers inside of her, that pussy locked onto my fingers greedily, it felt like her pussy was breathing and panting on my digits. Using the pad of my thumb, I rubbed her sensitive bud as I pushed my fingers in and out of her soppy wet tunnel.

Aubry let her head fall back, I kissed and licked her chin then ran my tongue down her throat. I couldn't stop now until I at least relieved her. Tears welled up in her eyes, I studied her face. Her mouth fell open, I picked up the pace.

"Relax baby and cum all over my fingers please." She slowly nodded her head and moaned a little too loudly. Shutting her up, I placed my mouth on top of hers and stole her breath away with my tongue sliding on top of her tongue. I flicked her bottom lip then sucked it into my mouth.

"When I finally get to eat this wet ass pussy, this is exactly how I'm going to treat it." I made sure to hit her G spot repeatedly. Her moaning in my mouth had my dick twitching and jerking. Aubry was the first woman to make my entire body heat the fuck up. The first woman to get me off without even entering her. She made me so sexually high that I felt tipsy as fuck. I traced her lips with my tongue, then sucked on her top and bottom lip. She started to shake violently as her eyes rolled back and her pussy clenched my digits even tighter.

"That's right, beautiful, give me all that shit." She bucked and panted until she fell limp up against me." I removed my fingers from her center and looked at my hand amazed by how wrinkled up my fingers were from playing in her pussy. Licking my hands clean, appreciating the fresh and clean taste of her pussy. I helped her to her seat behind her desk.

"You were telling me about the food baby, where is it?" I smirked as her eyes flickered open like she was desperately fighting to stay awake. I needed to get her to overcome the sexually induced coma that I put her in, so I went down to the hospital cafeteria to get her some coffee. I didn't want her bringing any attention to herself from her nosey ass coworkers.

Once she got the coffee that I bought her, I sat down and tore down the food that she had brought me from home. I already had plans on spoiling Aubry. I didn't want her falling for me from just the mind-blowing sex I could give her. I wanted her to fall for the man that could make her happy and add sex as a bonus.

PRINCESS

I sat across from my mom, staring at her blankly as she kept stealing glances of her nails as she talked on the phone to whom I assumed was my father's lawyer. I felt sad that I didn't have enough money to help pay for my father to get out of jail, but I guess my mom had the money and out of guilt she was going to make sure that my dad got out of jail. She didn't want to press charges, but they didn't care about any of that shit. My father was already considered a menace to society, and they were looking for any given excuse to throw him under a cell.

Shit like this is why I couldn't stop sniffing cocaine and smoking weed to ease my wicked reality of life. I hated my life but when I had the finer things and some good cocaine to toot up my nose I loved and dealt with it the best that I could. I couldn't hold secrets that well or even hide who I truly was. Doing cocaine was easy to hide because I still acted like myself, just probably moodier and wilder off the substance alone.

I had two weeks left in this substance abuse treatment program. I really had Logic to thank because this place had opened me up. I had a therapist, and I hadn't had any cravings go get high. Snorting cocaine had become normal for me for the past couple of years. It helped me zone out and sell myself whenever I entered the club to strip. It made me feel like that bitch and placed me on top of clouds. It made me move more seductively and feel more confident in myself. The way some men eyed me as I stripped was disgusting but if I was under the influence, I welcomed it knowing I would make a big check at the end of the night.

WITH COCAINE, it made me not give a fuck about shit and it kept my feelings frozen. Logic, Jaiden, and my brother Kane supported me a hundred percent. I also realized the true friend that I had in Jaiden. She was always selfless with me and poured into me without expecting something in return. I wanted to become a better person so that way I could become a better friend to Jaiden. I didn't want to lose her. I drummed my fingers against the table missing my nails.

Everything on me was plain down to my hair being slicked up into a ponytail.

"Damn, I'm so sick of talking to that fucking lawyer. I'd rather his ass stay in jail so I can have a stress-free pregnancy." I hadn't said shit to my mom about me knowing all about her and Histori fucking around. The thought alone made me sick to my core. I looked down at her baby bump and wanted to fucking throw up. That baby in her stomach was created by a man that I loved so much. I used to think once me and Histori got all the bullshit and games out of our systems that we would actually be together.

To think about him dicking down other bitches hurt me, but I got over it. To think about him fucking on my momma pained me to the core and made me start hating him. That was the nail in the coffin. I never wanted to see Histori face again or hear none of his lies.

"Why are you here, Patrice?" I eyed my momma like I wanted to jump across the table and beat her ass. She really had me fucked up and was very bold to even come up here and try to see about me. I didn't have to be told that my brother Kane told her where I was. Lately, all he had been talking about was peace amongst all of us, but I just wanted to be done with my mom all together. I didn't want shit to do with her.

"Don't disrespect me lil girl. I'm still your fuckin' momma and I will beat your ass like-"

"Disrespect you?" I raised my right brow and shook my head in disbelief.

"You really drove all the way to the boondocks still thinking that I will ever respect you when you never had it in you to render me the same type of fuckin' respect." I spat lowly.

"Bitch you ain't shit but an old dried-up hoe, wishing you was me. You just more stupid than me. You had to go and get pregnant by a nigga that just couldn't leave me alone since I was a kid." I chuckled and eyed her without blinking.

"You always tryna break me. I can be woman enough to tell you I ain't just bothered by it, you hurt me bad. You ain't my momma bitch and we ain't never got shit to talk about. You just a sick ass old bitter bitch that's in competition with me for no fucking reason. You aborted the other babies but kept this baby cause you ran out of ways to hurt me. Bitch I will never look at that bastard as my sister or brother just like I will never see you as my mother. Just a fucking bad ass surrogate."

"You lil fat ass bitch! WHO THE FUCK YOU THINK YOU TALKING TO? I'LL KILL YOU!" My mom stood to her feet, and I stood up right along with her. I was ready to stomp her like the roach she was.

"You already tried that, but I survived. Now you stuck with a bastard baby. You fenna be lonely as fuck, daddy ain't gone ever be back with you again. He gon' go find him somebody else and start a new and more improved family with. Hopefully he marry a new broad so I can call her momma and vibe out with her better than I was able to do with you. I might be a lot of things but I ain't never crossed you or tried to hurt you!" Tears were now streaming down my face as my entire body trembled from anger and hurt.

Staff approached our table and one of the security guards told my mom that she had to go. She started bucking and trying to get out of their grasp to run upon me, but she wasn't strong enough.

"Bitch FUCK YOU! I only came here to ask you if you seen my man!" She thought she ate with that so I laughed hard trying to wipe the tears from my eyes to clear my vision up, but they wouldn't stop coming.

"Bitch that nigga burning in hell! That baby in ya stomach was better off being aborted! You a single broke ass baby momma!" I felt myself being dragged away. I could hear chairs falling as my mom cursed and screamed trying her hardest to get to me. When I made it to my room, I lost my entire mind.

When I got to my room all I could see was red. Anything in sight I threw it and talked shit to myself why I destroyed the space around me.

"Fuckin' bitch! Old bitter ass bitch!" I picked up the folding table in my room and threw it hard against the door.

"Bitch tryna break me! Wanna see me down bad! Watch! I'm gon' flex on her ass!" In a blind rage, my eyes blurred with tears and my head started to thump. The need for a bump of cocaine took over me. The fact that I wasn't able to get to it or have the substance sent me tumbling down to the ground.

"Ahhhhhhhhhhhh!" I screamed at the top of my lungs. Kicking my feet like a toddler, I balled my fist and started hitting the center of my forehead.

"God! Please! Help me!" I rocked back and forth as I looked up at the off-white ceiling.

"I-I- I don't know what to do God! I don't even know why I am who I am and who the hell am I?" My sob got caught in my throat as I started to cough violently.

"God! I don't understand, why you keep giving me to people that don't love me." My heart ached as flashbacks of my entire life started popping up in my head. Every turn of event and even when I had done wrong haunted me. I couldn't count on one hand how many times I found myself truly happy. I constantly made excuses for myself because I didn't want to blame myself fully for never getting shit right and together. I had so much hate and hurt in my soul to the point of me not even wanting to be alive.

Histori popped up in my head and I hit myself even harder. I felt it, he was dead, and I wished he wasn't so I could be the one to fucking kill him and then myself. I wasted so much time on a man that didn't love and respect me enough. Out of all the females he slept with he decided to procreate with my mom. I couldn't be around her or even see that baby. It was a reminder of the ultimate betrayal. I never even processed it properly when Kane told me until today, when I saw her smug ass face staring at me like she finally succeeded at what she always sought out to do and that was what hurt me.

"God I'm broken! Just send me to hell. I can't do this anymore." I sniffled hard.

"You can do it and you will. Get yo ass up and stop making all that noise." My eyes snapped towards a thick tall chick. I saw her a couple of times in the facility and was told that she was one of the founders. Anytime I saw her she had this serious look plastered on her pretty face like she didn't take shit. A deep scar ran down the center of her forehead stopping at the bridge of her nose. It didn't take away from her beauty, it actually added to it.

"Please get out." She shut the door behind her ignoring what I just asked her. Stepping all the way inside her eyes roamed the mess I made. She bent down and picked up the folding table and placed it back in the center of my room.

"I won't be doing that. I don't take orders from any patient in my program. Now get off the floor and sit down in that chair so we can have a talk. My name is Markela by the way." I looked up into her brown eyes and frowned at her. She held her hand out and clicked her teeth like time was ticking. I grabbed her hand and stood up, when I was on my feet, I fell into her and hugged her tightly. I needed a hug, I needed to feel something right now. I needed my sanity more than anything.

Markela placed her hand on my back and rubbed it in circles.

"It's okay to feel the way that you feeling. At the end of this breakdown, you gotta think of ways to never feel this way again." I nodded my head slowly swallowing the painful lump in my throat.

"My mother, she-" Markela shook her head and pulled me away from her touching my shoulders.

"You gotta accept people for who the fuck they are and treat them accordingly baby girl. I live that way in life, it's how I protect my space and peace. Everybody might not like the way you are and who you are as a person. A lot of people will do you wrong and purposely try to hurt you. Once you feel that hurt and see how they really feel about you... You leave they fuck ass exactly where they stand. Make them stand on it and do you. All I see is weakness from you, you're vulnerable as hell and that is what probably landed you in this facility. Relying on substances to make you feel validated will keep you in a sunken place. Pitying yourself and begging God to take you away." She nodded her head towards the seat, and I went to sit down.

Markela picked up the other folding chair and sat right across from me.

"Can I smoke a cigarette?" Markela nodded her head. I didn't have to ask because they allowed us to smoke cigarettes in the facility. I got up and went to my plastic drawer and pulled out my lighter and Newport. Once I had it sparked, I took a seat holding my water bottle to use it as an ashtray. Markela pecked away at her iPhone as I sat calming myself down.

"I don't know who I am, I don't even know how to discover who I am." Markela didn't say shit for the first couple of seconds. Once she was done talking, she looked up at me and offered me a small smile.

"Be still. That's the start of finding yourself." She sighed then slid her phone into her bra.

"You have to be quiet, you cannot and will not be able to discover yourself until you take the time to be still. Realize who you truly are, not who you want to be. Find what you are good at, and not good at as well. Assess your relationships with people as well, it's also a huge part and reflection of the type of person you are. I only know from experience, me and you can be total opposites. I'm spoiled and the only child. Some love to call me a trust fund baby, unlike real trust fund babies who are wealthy, I still grind like I'm broke. I had so many people including my parents tending to my every need that I wasn't able to see myself crashing and I didn't know what to do once I finally did crash because I didn't know who the hell I truly was." She looked away from me at nothing in particular as she continued to talk. I listened closely because I desperately wanted to know how to better myself.

"I got this scar from a man that was jealous, insecure and every time I turned around… if he wasn't trying to hurt me physically, he was doing it verbally and emotionally. Don't get it fucked up, I use to hang with him on the physical side. I stayed because I didn't know my worth and I didn't know who the hell I was. You will be so surprised when you see that half of the world struggles with knowing who they are. When they see themselves in the mirror, they see what all they do for others and how they mold and become what other people want them to be. I learned how to practice radical self-acceptance after I detoxed myself of drug abuse, popping pills to escape my reality. Then I stayed still, spent time with myself." She chuckled softly then stared at me.

"My therapist told me that most people don't find themselves until they're like fifty years old, but I discovered me at twenty-five. As time went on, I let go of negative shit and negative self-talk. I focused on my strengths and stopped living in the past. The main thing that was a part of that was me stop giving a damn what other people thought of me. I cared about what I thought of myself. I start expressing how I truly felt and become honest with all of my responses which in return had people thinking that I was a bitch or very mean. See, I believe that there's a self-deep down that is consistent over time even with allowing change. You have to be able to recognize our identity as consistent, despite differences in actions or behaviors in specific contexts. The true self is that inner voice pulling us in the right direction. Everyone has that deep inner voice that tries to lead us in ways that are virtuous. Often times people beat that voice and train themselves to go in the wrong direction, so they end up losing that inner voice and then it becomes harder to even find and discover themselves. I'm talking so much because it's a beautiful ass thing to find yourself Princess and yes, I know your name. I know every person that comes in and out and some people I keep a watchful eye on."

I don't know why but chills came over me as I felt moved in a way I hadn't been moved by in so long. She held her hands out and I grabbed them as she looked deep into my eyes.

"Everything in life is temporary. The only constant in life is change itself. That is a reality that we cannot deny. The beauty of this fact is that it allows us to confront our fears, trust the magic of the moment, and enjoy the precious gift of life. What last forever is our true self...the real you... the person you were born to be no matter who had you. It does not matter how fucked up anybody has done you, including your mother. If you feel stuck, trapped, boring or insecure... acknowledge yourself, find yourself and who you really are on the inside. Your shiny sexy brilliant self is there, baby girl, and it's been there all along. You just have to be still and quiet to find it and stop shutting her out. Let her shine and lead the way and believe in it." She released my hands and stood up.

"I'll have my assistant bring you one of the notebooks I created so you can start journaling. It's called *Manifesting The Life You Want*. In that book you will do a lot of self-reflecting and noting different things down. Now when I give advice, I always say that's just me though... just in case you find yourself trying to blame me and the advice I give because it didn't go right for you." We both started laughing as she stood to her feet.

"Real talk baby girl, you are beautiful. I see very good things in you. I want you to see it too. The man who signed you up for my program is a good person as well. He gets on my employees' nerves because he calls three times a day to check in on you." That caused me to blush hard thinking about Logic. He was truly different, even more attentive than his father. Even if he and I didn't work out, I would want to keep him around as a friend for life like Jaiden. I enjoyed talking to Markela, she promised to have her assistant bring my journal when she got back in from her break.

When Markela left, I felt drained, but I felt better and foolish at the same time. Foolish because once again, I allowed my mother to get to me. I said a prayer and also promised myself to find the real me and connect with that person and do like Markela said, let it guide me and be proud of me.

JAIDEN

"Mommy, do we have to go to daddy house this weekend?" Jayla asked as she put one more barbie doll into her backpack.

"Yes Jayla, you have to go. That's your dad and he loves you just as much as I do. You don't want to hurt daddy feelings because you want to stay here with me, do you?" I was against talking bad about Rodrik to the kids. Even though the nigga got on my last nerves, I felt like he deserved a fair chance when it came to the girls.

"I'll go mommy, if I go, I'll get to get new toys from your best friend." I froze and frowned my face up.

"Who is my best friend?" I sat down on Jayla's twin bed, my stomach started to feel queasy.

"Nay Nay." I damn near fainted but kept my composure.

"Nayvius?" Jayla nodded her head.

"Yes, Nayvius. He comes to GG house to see me and Jaylen. Daddy don't like him; he frowns every time Nay Nay comes by to see us. I like Nay Nay, he always brings us cupcakes and ice cream. GG calls him a bitch and tells Daddy to stop being such a pussy." I bit down into my bottom lip to keep from laughing hard. Jayla was something else and the reason for that was any other time she talked like a little innocent toddler. Saying word for word what her grandmother said to Rodrik about Nayvius was clear. Jayla was five years old, so she still had her baby face and small squeaky voice. Most of the time it sounded like she was talking too fast, so it was hard to make out some of the things she said in sentence form.

Right now, she took her time to talk and spoke very clearly like she couldn't wait to recite what was said.

"Jayla, you do know that those words that your GG said were bad. Adults shouldn't use that kind of language. It makes them look ugly. Kids definitely can't use that kind of language either, you understand me?" She gave me that sad puppy dog look as I held my arms out for her to give me a hug.

I had a few slip ups with profanity but for the most part I did good with not cursing around them. I wanted my girls to have good behavior and manners. It started from home, which was another big reason that I hated them being at Rodrik's mom's house. This is what I now had to deal with since me and Rodrik were no longer together. I was okay with that, because there was nothing that a person could give me, that would make me take his triflin' lazy ass back.

These past months, I've been really doing me and enjoying being a single mom. It was like nothing changed; I didn't have a hard time adjusting. I always paid most of everything when Rodrik was here. I actually was able to save more money without him in the house with us. I didn't have to give him my last to buy his weed or buy all kinds of crazy snacks for when he had the munchies. There was no more guessing if he would break bread from his McDonald's checks either. All I had to do was take care of my girls and myself as well as the bills I had to pay. When I looked back on the pointless years of keeping Rodrik around, I saw the sacrifices I was willing to make and the ones he refused to make. I could go months without getting my feet, nails, and hair done.

Rodrik had to have weed, or his attitude would be shitty towards everyone in the house. I look back now and feel ashamed to even call him my baby daddy.

"I'm sorry mommy. I just don't really like being with Daddy and GG. It's fun but then it gets boring, daddy always play the game." I knew she wasn't lying which was why I was going to cut their time short from being over there. I stood up and told Jayla to give me a minute so I could call her dad and have a talk to him. I was even surprised that Rodrik hadn't come crying to me about Nayvius crazy ass popping up over there.

On the way to my room, I unblocked Nayvius' number and sent him a text telling him that we needed to talk. Next, I called Rodrik and braced myself for the bullshit because that's all his ass ever dished out when it came to us communicating like adults.

"What's up Jaiden." He sounded calm, which was new.

"Hey Rodrik, I wanted to ask if it's okay that the girls spend one night with you, if they decide to stay the weekend that's fine too. Jayla say she be bored because you're constantly on the game while they are there." I shut my eyes waiting for his shitty response that I knew was coming.

"Well, my girl bought Disneyland resort tickets. I forgot to let you know that we were going to spend the weekend in Orange County." I could hear the smirk in his voice like he had succeeded in pissing me off.

"Oh okay, the girls would love that. I'm pretty sure they will be fine staying with you the entire weekend now. My only thing now is meeting this woman that you're going to have around my kids." Rodrik had me fucked up thinking that I was going to be fine with my kids around a total stranger that I never met.

"I don't think that's even necessary, Jaiden. You been having this nigga Nayvius around our girls for months now without even asking me."

"No, I haven't..." I bit into my bottom lip, I made another mental note to just pop up on Nayvius ass and let him have it. I didn't know what his deal was but then again, I kind of did... An alarm set off in my head as I thought back to a conversation me and Nay had.

"I haven't fucked Rodrik in a long time. We are not together right now." I cut my eyes hard at him.

"Right now, huh? You ain't never getting back with him since I'm involved." He put me down to my feet.

"I think you already know I'm crazy as fuck. After I get this pussy...." He cupped my camel toe and smiled like he was crazy.

"I'll be popping up at your house, school and wherever else I want to be when I want to see you. I know that lil hoe friend of yours pillow-talked with you. I ain't clearing shit up, that's what you was getting at when we was having dinner asking me what I did for a living. Just know, Jaiden... you all in my personal space where I lay my head at. I know you heart broken and I ain't no rebound ass nigga. Right now, I want to be the nigga to eat the fuck out of your pussy, rub your feet while I deep stroke the fuck out of yo shit. By the time I'm done with you, you gone walk funny and act funny with any nigga that even try to spit game or look at you. Come on let's shower, sweat don't bother me when I'm fucking but I need the pussy fresh when I taste it." Lord, what was I getting myself into.

"Look Rodrik... I don't know what you and Nayvius have going on. Obviously, you let him come around instead of standing up to him. That has nothing to do with me and everything to do with your bitch-ass-ness." I couldn't even contain the fit of giggles that left my mouth.

"I ain't no bitch! I just got a lot to live for!" He yelled into the phone.

"Oh, okay, so you are scared. That's understandable... again it has nothing to do with me. If you're scared of Nayvius and if he's there and not welcomed, then you and your mom should call the police." I felt my stomach getting super queasy. The urge to throw up took over me as I tried my best to swallow the shit down. For the past couple of weeks nauseousness had started to come and go.

"If you want to meet her, you come drop the kids off." Rodrik gave in surprisingly fast, I wondered if Nayvius was the reason behind that. Even all of Rodrik's threats about taking me to court stopped. He normally would keep the arguing going and I would have to hang up in his face to end the madness.

"I sure will drop them off." I hung up the phone in his face not wanting to talk any longer. My stomach tightened again, and I had to run to the bathroom this time to puke my guts up. My body felt cold all over and sweat formed on my forehead.

"Shit, I'm coming down with a bad bug." After brushing my teeth, I heard loud banging on my door. Not expecting anyone, my stomach knotted up again as anxiety started to get the best of me.

"Jayla, Jaylen... stay in y'all room." The knocking persisted as I picked up my pace on my way to the front door.

"Who is it?" I shouted.

"You wanted to talk." Nayvius' deep husky voice sounded

off as I stepped back from the door, astonished that he drove his ass to my house.

"You finally unblocked a nigga… You did that shit just in enough time Jai. I warned you what it was with me and then I went against my own fuckin' warnings and gave yo silly ass space Ma." Oh shit, this nigga really was insane.

"I meant for us to talk over the phone." Nayvius laughed loudly, I opened the door and connected with his wild eyes. His blind gray eye was the first eye I always saw first. He licked his two-toned cinnamon and pink lips and leaned against my door frame.

"You wanted to talk baby… A nigga misses you badly. I been taken time out to get to know the kids, so I won't go and do all the things I warned you about, like popping up at your school and job… now here."

"Nayvius, this is not-"

"Nay… I love when you call me fucking Nay now Jai." I hated that Nayvius was so damn fine. Like the type of fine that instantly make your pussy thump and come alive with a constant pulse.

"You look so fucking good. I can't believe you stayed away from me for months and to think that I actually allowed that shit." He tucked his bottom lip into his mouth.

"Nayvius, you been bullying the father of my kids." His face darkened, scaring me, and making me regret revealing that to him.

"His bitch ass said something to you?" He stood up off the door frame and cracked his knuckles.

"No, Jayla told me how you're there when they are there which is not a good thing. That's like imposing and forcing your way into my daughter's life." I crossed my arms over my breast.

"No, it's not baby. It's called speeding up the process. I

gotta get to know them and love them since I feel that way about their momma. You been raising them right too, they some really good ass kids. I didn't ask you because then you would say no. So, I stopped by Rodrik momma house, and he said that the shit was fine. He even calls me every time they're over there. So, you see, I got one parents permission." I shook my head no, as Nayvius shook his head yes.

"Jaiden, you gotta be more careful who you decide to open those thick ass thighs too. A nigga like me ain't coming up off of you easily. I gave you space, so I didn't scare you. All I really want to do is make your life easier."

"How do you plan on doing that Nay? By fucking me in the middle of the night then up and leaving me to go Lord knows where? I'm not that kind of woman and I will not let you handle me that way."

"You right as fuck baby. I know you not that kind of woman. That's why I want to stand on business when it comes to you. I want to make your life easier by eating that pussy daily, sending you out of my house with a smile everyday while you grind and do ya thang. I mean you don't have to grind but I know you like staying on top of ya shit. So, I'll support you with that. Most of all, I'm gone be the best step daddy ever. I already learned so much about the girls." He stepped up close to me, pulling me in by the waist.

I didn't push him back, it seemed like he needed this hug just as bad as I did. Wrapping my arms around him, he placed his chin on top of my head then rubbed my back until his hands fell to the cuff of my ass.

"I been going through some shit Jaiden. Some tough shit but I've been getting through it. I see so much light in you, you shared your light without me even asking for it. Making me want to do and be better so I can forever be a part of you."

I pulled back and looked into his eyes, I was getting ready

to say something but stopped when I saw his eyes well up with tears. I never in my life saw a man so vulnerable but seeing Nayvius like this made my heart ache for him. Behind those wild eyes of his showed strength, courage as well as a sad ass story that he was holding back from telling.

"Come in Nayvius so we can really talk." I grabbed his hand and led him down the hall to my room.

NAYVIUS

"Thugs cry too, Jai." I lowered my head and chuckled. That was the only way that I knew how to manage the agony of pain that I felt every day. I never wanted to open up to anyone and tell a person just how I truly felt. For some reason when I looked into Jaiden's eyes, I felt safe. Like I could tell her my deepest secrets and feel secure in knowing that she wouldn't use that shit against me.

"Be serious Nay, I want to know what's hurting. I kind of have an idea, but I want you to express it out loud. It's clear that you hold it in and that is not healthy." I nodded my head, hating that I was feeling so emotional right now. When Jaiden texted me, telling me that we needed to talk. I was at my childhood home battling myself. I had been sober from opening up a bottle of liquor, the weed just wasn't helping me with coping so I tried to find some type of strength to ignore my need to get pissy drunk.

"I've gone years minimizing the loss of both parents. I know that if I really look deep into it, I only come up with one answer. It being my fault. I mean I stressed them out so fucking bad Jai... Hustling... being in the fucking streets when I didn't have to be. I remember coming in late, seeing my momma's eyes puffy from crying worrying about me and if I would make it to see another day. My father loved me deeply, but he started to fuckin' hate me because of all the stress I put onto my momma. I wasn't like most niggas, having to get shit out the mud to survive. I had two parents working hard and trying their best to raise me to be the best that I could be. I don't even know why I turned to fast money. It was easy, it came with respect and niggas bowing down to me when they saw me. I guess that shit was like an adrenaline rush that I had become addicted to." I laid back on Jaiden's bed not being able to look her in the eyes right now as tears streamed out the corners of my eyes into my ears. I started on the day that I lost my parents.

"Nayvius! Don't you turn your back and walk out of this house! I won't tolerate you disrespecting me any longer!" I turned to look at my mom, as bad as I wanted to stop from walking out of that door I couldn't. I had to be front in center to collect payments from all the Kingpins today. Midas was my boy, but we hadn't known each other that long to be playing around with money.

Yesterday my father had gon' through my shit, but it was all my fault for him finding it. I should have taken it to the safe house. For that reason alone, he flushed that shit down and for the first time ever I fought him hard like he was a nigga off the streets. When I broke the story down to Midas, he was cool with it but suggested that I move smarter next time. I paid him back for the bricks that were supposed to go to one of the Kingpins on the southside and today I had to make the drop.

I should have moved out of my parent's house, I just loved coming home to meals and being here under my momma. Whenever I did say that I was leaving she begged me to stay. I hated that my mom worried so much. I was doing this to make their lives easier. My father was working construction and complained about his back hurting all the time. My mom worked as well but I could always see how tired she was.

I hated that I was rolling around living carefree making fast money and had enough to take care of my parents. They just wouldn't accept or take a dollar from me, not wanting to condone my illegal way of living.

"Let the nigga leave! I won't have you stressing over his fuck ups anymore. We tried hard enough and today that trying stops. I done put myself into lots of debt! I put up the house to bail your ass out! I've washed my hands with you boy!" My father's voice boomed as he looked over at me with so much fury and hate.

"I'm a grown ass man! Nobody told you to set bail for me. What you want the money back? I tried to give you that shit!" I yelled back, I regretted even yelling because now my mom started crying harder as she turned to my father.

"Sr. we can't ever give up on our boy baby."

"He's a grown ass man! I owe a big ass gambling debt! I'm running out of ideas to show this young and dumb ass nigga the stress that he is causing in my damn household! Now he's grown Naleah! A grown ass man that thinks he can do whatever he wants! He has got to do that shit outside of this house so we can finally live and do what married couples do at this age."

"You right Pops... I apologize and if you let me pay you back for your troubles, I will be on my way."

"I don't want a cent of your money boy. One day you will see that none of this was worth it. Living the way that you live will land you in jail or a fuckin' grave. Now you making your bed son, your mom and I love you but it's time we let you lay

in the bed that you keep remaking. I can't have my wife losing anymore sleep behind-"

Ratatattat! Gun shots rang out, I tried to run to cover my mom but got hit in the eye. I got hit in the shoulder and felt myself in and out of consciousness but held on for dear life praying that we all made it out of this shit. I never remembered praying so hard in my life.

When the ambulance got to my parents' house, I looked over and saw holes all in my father's back. He was lying on top of my mother dying to protect her. They took me to the hospital and kept me highly sedated to perform surgeries on me. They told me that my parents didn't make it and by the time I got out the hospital, my family had planned their funeral without telling me shit.

Midas had given me the information to where their services were held. I made sure to let my family know that they were dead to me as well. I stayed at their gravesite for days crying and drinking until I felt numb and delirious. I found the niggas that were responsible for killing them and went into overkill. I thought it would make me feel better, but it didn't.

Jaiden was laying on my chest crying as she rubbed my head. My chest tightened and a low sob that rose from my throat left my mouth.

"I tried to blame my dad because he should've let me pay him back so he could pay whoever he owed money too. In the end I blame myself because if they weren't so worried about my stupid ass, they'd still be alive. I don't have no family, I got Midas but ain't shit like having your parents. The same family that blames me for the loss of my parents is the same family that only calls me when they are in a bind, and I give them what they want out of guilt thinking that one day they will accept me. Especially my momma sister who looks just like my fuckin' momma. I don't know that shit turned me into something that I never thought that I would be. Killing without feeling and feeding off the shit so I don't have to feel all this pain that has been consuming me for the past five years." I sat up and swallowed down the lump of pain that formed in my throat.

"Holding onto remorse can prevent you from reaching the acceptance phase of grief. Nayvius..." Jaiden sat up and looked me in the eyes, her loving eyes calmed me down as she pecked me on the chin, lips then nose.

"You can't keep this cycle of guilt inside of you. You know that they are gone but you haven't accepted it due to all of this remorse. That last conversation you had with them is still stuck in your brain. Self-blaming leads to feeling isolated and lonely. You have to reach out for help and support and let your thoughts and voice be heard. You cannot keep it bottled in and you should think about changing your way of life Nay. That lifestyle is not promised, and if you allow yourself to grow and heal you will see clearer. Your parents are waiting for you to do the right thing. Once you accept their death and allow yourself to properly grieve, it should encourage you to want to live right."

My chest tightened as I welcomed the silence and replayed her words in my head. I never saw shit that way. I used my way of living as an outlet. Anytime I went and killed a muthafucka for testing my nuts, I thought about how a pussy nigga took my parents away. I used that shit as fuel to take lives away because it made me feel a little better. I used alcohol as my crutch because it made shit numb.

What Jaiden had said made lots of fucking sense, Midas mentioned change as well and I was opened to it. I had enough money tucked away. If I didn't want to work ever again in my life, I could do that. I wanted to invest and get into something that would make my parents proud of me.

"I want to open a construction company. My dad loved building. In honor of him, I want to start a company that builds houses, maybe even mansions and big ass companies." I saw excitement in Jaiden's eyes as her pretty blue eyes twinkled and shined with so much light.

"That would be so dope Nay. You gotta let me help you plan that-" She stopped talking and hopped up off her ass like something had burned her. She ran to the bathroom and started throwing up causing me to sit up and snap out of our intimate moment. I wasn't that fuckin' smart, but I knew for a fact that females only threw up from either being too drunk, or eating some shit that didn't agree with them or.... Pregnancy." I stood up off the bed and walked into Jaiden's bathroom just as she turned on the sink water to brush her teeth.

"Jai, you trying to get a nigga killed huh?" My chest ached as fear clutched me tightly.

"What the hell are you talking about Nayvius?"

"Why you calling me that now?"

"Nigga it's your name right? Look, I have to go take the girls to Rodrik's house so I can meet his new girlfriend before they take them to the Disneyland resort." I walked all the way into the bathroom and stood behind her wrapping my arms around her waist. She blushed hard then giggled.

"Ain't shit funny about death Jaiden. You better hope you ain't throwing up because you let another nigga get all inside of my shit." She playfully slapped my hands away then laughed.

"Nay you are really crazy. The last man I had sex with was you, and we used protection! Are you staying or coming with me while I go take the girls." I big smile crossed my face as I placed a big kiss in the nook of her neck.

"Now you want me around the girls." That shit made me feel good.

"Uhhh yea, well you already been around them creep. So, they know you so now I feel comfortable with you being around them."

"Yea alright, let's roll then." I walked out the bathroom, pulling my phone out and going straight to google. I plopped down on Jaiden's couch and searched Bath Basins for adults, I found the perfect one at Walmart that could fit into Jaiden's toilet so I could get samples of her pee. I added a couple of pregnancy tests along with the Bath Basin. If I was the last nigga she fucked and if she was pregnant with my baby, then she would have no choice but to accept the help that I wanted to give her to upgrade her and the girls.

I placed the order with Walmart that said same day delivery. When Jaiden, Jayla, and Jaylen walked into the living room. Both girls ran full speed towards me and hugged me tightly.

"Nay Nay!!!! Finally, you come to mommy house!" Jayla the oldest hugged my neck tightly. I could feel little Jaylen hugging my leg." When Jayla let go, Jaylen held her tiny hands out.

"Up, up!" I stood and swooped her in my arms. This right here felt different, it got to me and made me feel like I had a chance at real love. Pure love with no judgment. I looked over and saw Jaiden looking over at us like she was in shock. I really wasn't on no bullshit when I first started popping up at that nigga Rodrik house.

He was a lazy ass nigga, selfish as fuck, and didn't give a damn about putting forth an effort. Jaiden went through enough with him, and I didn't want him becoming a stress factor to her. So, I straightened that nigga out, I didn't give

him any options. If he wanted to be involved with these innocent girls, then he had to step up and be a real father.

I didn't know much about being a dad, but I never forgot
how well my father raised me. All the time my father spent
with me, teaching me things that I would never forget. From
what I observed, Jayla and Jaylen loved their dad, and they
wanted that niggas attention. Kids hardly ever saw the imper-
fection of their parents' they just wanted to be loved.

"I told you; I was mommy best friend." I looked over at
Jaiden rolling her eyes and smirked at her.

"I love you as mommy best friend." Jayla looked a lot
like Jaiden, her little chubby cheeks, nose, and eyes had
Jaiden written all over.

"Okay guys let's go." Jaiden picked up her keys just as I
stopped her from walking towards the door.

"You gotta go change first." I eyed Jaiden hard; she
looked juicy as hell. She liked wearing them damn leggings
that showed the curve of her thick ass thighs and butt. She
had on a graphic Tupac shirt but made sure the shirt was
sitting above her ass.

"Best friends don't tell each other what to wear." Jaiden
giggled but I didn't find shit funny.

"Well girls, looks like I'm mommy best friend and
boyfriend."

"Nay!" Jaiden looked like she wanted to hit me.

"It's true Jayla and Jaylen, are y'all okay with me being
mommy's boyfriend? She mean a lot to me and I will always
make her happy." Jaylen didn't understand anything I was
saying. She talked in her baby talk and smiled like she
understood.

"Yes! Then me and Jay Jay will have two daddies!" I
nodded my head and smiled.

"Yeap two dads, now Jai, go change into something

comfortable." Jaiden smacked her lips but there was no hiding all the blushing that she did when she saw how protective I was of her. She didn't even argue with me, she sat her keys down and went to go change. I wasn't putting shit past Rodrik, and if I caught that nigga staring at my woman's ass, I'd break his fucking neck.

I made the girls sit on the couch as I grabbed Jaiden's keys to grab Jaylen's car seat out of her car. I definitely planned on getting Jaiden, a more reliable car. The first step was getting her up out of this bad neighborhood.

I couldn't wait to really go full force into this. I still had shit on the backend to wrap up. Having the talk that I had with Jaiden was the beginning of something new. I imagined how unhappy my parents were with me, watching me from heaven. I still hadn't made any major changes, but I was now determined to do that shit.

Building a relationship with Jaiden and her kids already felt like it would be deeply fulfilling for me. I was already understanding, I had patience when it came to her and them and I was willing to start a family and put in the work with them. Jaiden wasn't out here in the streets like most chicks were. She was a beautiful soul in and out. She had her shit together, strong, and dependable. She knows what she wants and makes that shit clear and she knows how to give and receive love, not making shit a one-way street.

After I had the car seat properly put into my back seat, Jaiden and the girls were walking towards my car.

"This is going to be my family." I thought out loud and couldn't hold back the smile etched on my face. Jaiden put on some sweats with the same graphic shirt, and I couldn't hold in my laugh. Now her ass was being funny, but I didn't mind her wearing baggy ass clothes around her baby daddy. Jaiden was fine as fuck; it was a plus that she knew exactly how fine her ass was.

I put on music that was age appropriate for the kids and even that had me shocked. I already started to adapt and get used to having kids around me.

"We got a lot of catching up to do this weekend." I reached over and squeezed Jaiden's thigh.

"Oh, I'm spending the weekend with you?"

"Why wouldn't you be? We made up, we had the last bit of time apart that we are going to ever have away from each other again." I glanced over at her and winked.

"Yea okay… we still taking things slow." She turned and looked at the girls in the back seat.

"Seem like things will be speeding up, with the way you have been throwing up. I'll get to the bottom of it pretty soon." I glanced at her stomach then placed my eyes back on the road. Letting my hand travel from her thigh to her stomach, I gave it a light squeeze and to me, it felt hard. If Jaiden was pregnant with my baby that would actually seal the deal for both of us.

That would only make it clear to me that she was meant for me. It would also make me happy as hell. I wasn't worried about the time frame of knowing her. I felt like she was the one the moment that I laid eyes on her even though she tried to give me a hard ass time by claiming that lame ass nigga Rodrik.

"I want to holler at you really quick." She lifted up the big frames that covered her face and my heart damn near stopped. It was rare that you saw a caramel chick with blue eyes. Nah, those had to be contacts but dammit they looked real as fuck. For the first time and a long time, I didn't know what the fuck to say.

I probably looked goofy as fuck standing in the entryway of this liquor store blocking her path asking to holler at her.

"You don't got shit to holler at me about. You don't know me, and I damn sure don't know you. If you tryna get some pussy, that's off the menu too. I have a nigga and two kids at home. Excuse me." Even her voice was soft and sexy. She had on a dingy-ass Nike shirt with some black Nike sandals that looked like she placed them on her feet every day. Placing her shades back on, she sidestepped me and walked right out of the store.

I followed right behind her, looking down at her ass. That shit had a mind of its own.

"You got a nigga but he making you walk and shit."

"That ain't none of your concern. I just told you, I have two kids and they need they daddy. I ain't fucking up my family for you."

"I don't want to fuck up your family baby. I just want to get to know you as a friend. Talk to you on the phone and see how your day going. I'm never pressed about pussy." Her eyes squeezed into thin slits.

"You not gon' let me go on about my day are you?" she shook her head and smiled. Got dammit, this bitch had deep-dish dimples.

"I can't do that at all. What's your name?" She rolled her eyes and leaned all her weight onto her other leg.

"Jaiden." She batted her curly lashes. What women didn't understand was that niggas appreciated raw natural beauty. If I was to ever make her mine, at least I got to see right now how she would look lounging around the house in her natural state. Her smooth caramel face was blemish-free. She had pouty pink lips and even though she was dressed down with leggings and a dingy-ass shirt, she smelled good as fuck.

"Jaiden, yo nigga just don't know what he got, do he?"

"He does." She didn't sound too convincing. I didn't even understand myself right now. I started this conversation from jump in an attempt to add her to my roster of bitches. Her short feisty thick ass took me by surprise when I got up close and really saw her.

"He don't, pretty ass girl. I can tell by the way your voice dropped that you know that nigga laid up in your house comfortable as fuck. He probably thinks don't nobody else want your fine ass. Got you making store runs by yourself walking the streets. He doesn't even know a cold nigga like me, ready to snatch you the fuck up and make you feel some things you ain't never felt before. Deep in your core and in yo fucking mind baby." I stepped into her personal space, and she didn't flinch.

"I see you through both eyes. That's saying a lot when one of my eyes don't even see clearly. I see you baby, and ain't tryna waste your time. You probably content with your situation at home like I'm content with keeping bitches in rotation. I just want to be your friend though, a nigga you call and a nigga that's willing to listen. Hopefully, you can listen to me too. We can be each other's listening ear." I ran my hand down her waist and pulled back before she could reject me.

I could see the battle evident on her face. Never in my life have I felt this type of pull with any chick I approached. There were layers to this woman. Layers that were tough to peel back.

"Give me your number, Jaiden." I pulled my phone out and handed it to her. No was not an option. She was a light that shined through my darkness. Today was meant to be a dark and depressing day. I was already halfway done with my fifth of Hennessy and now I had sobered up.

I watched her delicate fingers punch her number in my

phone. When she handed it back our hands touched. A feeling of alignment between us took place. It felt like we were on the same wavelength. She didn't appear as a stranger, and I didn't want to leave her presence.

"What's your name?" She asked as I pressed call on the number, she punched in.

"Nayvius."

"Okay Nayvius, like I said I do have a man. As long as you respect that we can associate with one another." I chuckled lowly, licking my lips.

"Baby, if you were really dedicated to that nigga... you wouldn't have even entertained me for this long." I put my phone into my back pocket once I confirmed that she gave me the right number.

"I think we soulmates, but I'll respect your so-called relationship for now." I moved in on her, pecking her on the forehead and walking away. Jaiden was going to be mine. I was going to make it my mission to peel all those layers back and bust her ass wide open.

"Yea I definitely busted that ass wide open. Done fucked around and fell in love with a pretty ass BBW and got her pretty ass pregnant." I chuckled talking under my breath.

"What you say, Nay?" I tried to hold back the big ass grin but couldn't help that shit. Jaiden's ass probably turning red in the face. That's how blown she had me over her. I laughed like she had me nervous. Shit all of this had me kind of stuck. My initial plan wasn't this with Jaiden. Then I noticed how I wanted to be damn near close to perfect so that she can see the good in me. She made me feel like I could be myself. Not once did she make none of this about what all I could do for her.

I wanted to spoil Jaiden, make her feel secure with me. I

wanted to help her by showing her what it was like to have a real nigga that really wanted to fuck with her the long way.

"You heard what I said." I wanted to lean over and kiss her but remember we had the girls in the back seat. I couldn't wait to get her fine thick ass alone. Jaiden always smelled so fucking good, making me want to live in her damn skin all day.

JAIDEN

J woke up at Nayvius house smelling burned bacon and loud rap music playing loudly from down the hallway. Sitting up in bed, I felt sore. It was a good sore, the kind of sore that made me think about everything we did last night.

We had another deep talk and after that talk, he made love to me than fucked me hard. Nayvius was a gentle giant when it came to me. The way he listened when I talked, made jokes just to see me smile. He handled my body like he knew it better than me.

I could hear him shouting out the lyrics to Future's song, "Wait For You" I assumed, he was in there cooking me up some breakfast because last night he promised he would cook for me then take me out for the day. I slowly got out of his king size bed and stretched, looking around his cozy room.

For Nayvius to be a man, he was well organized and clean. I loved that; his house smelled like incense mixed with his cologne. I went straight to the bathroom to pee and handle my hygiene.

Sitting down on the toilet, I noticed that my pee was actually splashing real close to my damn pussy. When I finished, I stood up and frowned as I looked down at the toilet.

"A Bath Basin?" I couldn't even take my eyes off of it as I jumped to the sound of Nayvius voice behind me.

"Good morning baby." Nayvius had on black latex gloves like he was getting ready to perform a procedure on me. Digging in his basketball shorts, I admired his hard rock body. Nayvius was tatted all over in the right places and I liked that he didn't cover his eight-pack with tatts. His skin was smooth and blemish-free except for his arms and hands which had scars and cuts.

"So, I'm going to use all three of these tests. Hand me that Basin." He placed the three-pregnancy test down on the bathroom sink. I was too stunned to say anything.

"You really think I'm pregnant?" I couldn't believe Nayvius right now, I carefully handed him the Basin that was full of my pee.

"I'm new and true to this baby." He winked at me while sitting the Basin down onto the counter. He put his back to me as he focused on doing the test. I took that time to start some shower water to keep my nervousness together. A whole damn baby? My feelings were growing for Nayvius, but we were clearly still in the beginning stages.

Panic seeped into my pores as I tried to foresee the future between the both of us. I was not ready for another kid, but I would have no choice but to get ready if I was. I didn't have to ask Nayvius if he would be there for his baby because the way he handled my daughters without even knowing them fully spoke volumes. I also let the whole not knowing each other well shit fly out the window when we dropped the girls off at Rodrik's mother house.

Nayvius walked right into that house with me, leading the way. The way he asked questions and checked to see if I was okay with things made me fall for him even more. He just had big dick energy. Nayvius was all man, from his head down to his crooked toes. The way we picked up like we never stopped talking showed the true chemistry we had between one another.

The shower door slid open, and Nayvius stepped in looking at me with glossy eyes.

"Thank you, baby." He bowed his head, swiping underneath his eyes to try to stop his tears from falling.

"A nigga always wanted a family. Like a real ass family. Losing my parents made me feel like I was all alone in this world. Like when I get done doing what all I do for the day, I come home to silence. Some days, I'm cool with that shit, other days it gets to me and then I start trying to get high or drunk. I don't care about the timing or how fast we moving shit. I want this Jaiden; I swear you will never feel the way that nigga made you feel with me." He grabbed my hands and pulled me close until my breasts were pressed up against his midsection.

I looked up into his eyes and my emotions were raw. My throat started to burn and so were my eyes.

"I want this, I want you. I might be a lil crazy, but I don't mean no harm." I nodded my head, unable to formulate words right now. All of what he was saying gave me my answer. I was pregnant, all of those test came back positive. Looking into Nayvius' eyes my eyes always locked in on his blind eye. It always seemed like he had no problem seeing out of that eye from the way that he stared back at me and the way that he carried himself.

"I see you through both eyes. That's saying a lot when one of my eyes don't even see clearly. I see you baby, and ain't tryna waste your time. You probably content with your situation at home like I'm content with keeping bitches in

rotation. I just want to be your friend though, a nigga you call and a nigga that's willing to listen. Hopefully, you can listen to me too. We can be each other's listening ear."

"I'm the only woman you can see with both eyes?" I smiled as he picked up my left hand and started kissing my fingertips.

"Clear as a muthafucka, I ain't even looking at hoes with my good eye baby." He chuckled, always turning a serious moment into a laughing one.

"I can work with imperfections and mistakes. What I won't work with is poor decisions, Nay. I'm not that woman that will stay with you after you claim you made a mistake and cheated because that's a decision not a mistake. I want us open and honest with each other. I want to feel and know you care and want this; I don't want to ask I want to see it. I don't want to ever feel like we are just existing and making some shit work for the kids' sake. I want to be happy with you... I'm already happy with who I am so I don't have to depend on you to give me happiness, but I expect you to add on to that happiness like I will add on to yours. We work together through anything and grow together and show the kids what true love and dedication looks like. I pour into you... you pour into me." I laid it out confidently.

I didn't plan on wasting my time any longer. I already knew how I felt about Nayvius, and I didn't want to let him go. I wanted to lay things out so he could already know what I expected, and I wanted him to feel secure in knowing that I would make him feel just as good.

"We working towards marriage like my parent's Jaiden. I want our son to know how to be a real man. You're the perfect example of what a real woman should be like. It ain't gone take me years to realize that you're the woman that I need to wife up. So, trust me when I say, I'm on what you on." He gives me this assessing look like he's trying to read me by studying my face.

Nayvius grabbed underneath my thick thigh and lifted it up as he aligned his dick with the entrance of my pussy and entered me slowly.

"We can keep talking but I gotta be inside of you inside of this shower baby. I mean I get into some water and start thinking about how wet this pussy gets for me. Then you gone be living here, cooking for me... looking sexy as fuck even when you think you looking fucked up." The way he hit my G spot like it was target practice was starting to make me oblivious as he grunted and talked hot shit right into my ear canal.

He held onto the bottom of my ass, helping me maintain my balance as he tailgated this pussy.

"Take all this dick, Jaiden." He bit down onto my shoulder, speeding up his feral pumps. The arch in my back deepened as the water wet my face up making me close my eyes. *Smack!* He slapped me hard on the ass and pulled halfway out the drove all the way into the hilt of my pussy.

Nayvius moved so fast, the next thing I knew he was on his knees with my swollen clit in his mouth. I blushed at the sight of him holding my stomach up like it was in the way of him putting my entire pussy into his mouth. Swirling his tongue around my clit with the right amount of pressure had my eyes rolling back. My nipples stiffened as I started to pinch and rub them between my fingers enjoying the extra stimulation.

I rotated my hips and thrust forward, grinding right into his mouth as he stopped me by spreading my southern lips then sticking his thick long tongue in and out of my sticky tunnel.

"Agh, fuck Nay!" I started to shake as my entire body trembled.

Tracing his tongue all the way back to my clit, he kissed at it as if he were kissing my lips. He was well acquainted with my pussy as well as my body, there was no hesitation when he ate my pussy. He did it exactly how I liked and knew when I was close to climaxing. A streak of jealousy had me moaning and rolling my eyes thinking about other females that got the chance to experience this side of Nayvius.

He was a certified freak; he wouldn't nut unless he had me cumming more times than I could count. Whenever he was eating or inside of me, he had me forgetting exactly who the hell I was.

I tried to move away from him as I started to cum, but he grabbed both ass cheeks and brought me closer. He started to act a fool in my pussy making sure I wet up his entire damn face by shaking his head from side to side. When my shaking stopped, he sucked my clit softly applying the right amount of pressure to get my pussy aroused all over again.

He stood to his feet and kissed me deeply, snatching my soul away from my body, making it tie into his. I gasped at Nayvius lifting me up off my feet with my legs locked into his arms. Smoothly sliding his dick deep inside of me, he looked me into my eyes and sighed hard.

"You gon' have me slipping and sliding all up in this fuckin' shower." He smirked, turning me until my back was up against the shower glass. I relaxed and accepted his girth deep inside of me. Nayvius dick was long and thick, it filled me to the brim, like he was molding my pussy to adapt to his dick.

"Shit baby." He gritted digging in and out as he continued to stretch my walls. Holding onto his shoulders, I bit into my bottom lip and stayed still as I let him fuck my pussy and take it however, he wanted it. Just by locking eyes with him felt magical, it felt so right like our bond was growing deeper and deeper.

"Rock your hips baby, fuck a nigga back and show me how much you want this dick." He held onto me like I weighed absolutely nothing. Each time me and Nay fucked, it felt like the very first time. I slowly rocked my hips matching each thrust he delivered. Nayvius leaned in and started sucking my nipples with the right amount of pressure, making my pussy tightened around his girth with need.

"Fuck baby, I love you!" Nayvius breathed huskily as my eyes began to flutter.

"I love you too Nay." I moaned, feeling myself about to reach another orgasm.

"You better fuckin' love me forever, this pussy belongs to me. I mean that shit." His wild eyes didn't blink once as his veins popped out of his forehead, neck. I now became determined to throw this pussy back a little faster and harder on him. I wanted him just as sprung as he was making me. Nayvius gazed into my eyes as he licked his sexy full lips.

"Come on, I gotta see how you ride." I guess we were skipping soaping up our bodies. Grabbing me by the throat, then covering my lips with his had me inhaling sharply, as he slapped me on the ass and opened the shower door for me to step out. I walked out of Nayvius bathroom dripping wet with him following closely behind.

I was a little rusty when it came to riding dick, but that voice inside of my head was screaming, *Put the pussy on this nigga and make him fall deeper in love with you, Jaiden!* Smirking to myself, Nayvius laid on the bed and placed his hands behind his head cockily. The look on his face pulled at my heartstrings. He looked at me with so much passion and desire that it had me turned on to the max.

I focused on his dick standing up at attention, veins decorating his long length, my mouth started to water as precum oozed out of the tip. I wanted to take control and hear his husky moans. I wanted to give him the same euphoric intense pleasure that he gave me.

Crawling on the bed making sure to arch my back so he can see my ass from the front, I lowered my lips until my breath fanned the pink mushroom tip of his dick. I pressed hot, open mouth kisses to the tip then licked down his shaft making sure to get his entire dick wet. Grabbing his dick with both hands, I twisted it and jacked it up and down then licked around the rim of his head where his sensitive nerves were.

"Fuck baby, you posed to be riding. You sucking that shit, fuck! You look so fucking sexy baby." His words were coming out choppy as he took deep breaths. That shit boosted my confidence as I engulfed his entire dick into my mouth, relaxing my throat and breathing through my nose, I took him until he was going past my tonsils.

"Ohhh shit!" he sat up and grabbed a handful of my hair, I zoned out and went to work on his dick until I felt it twitching. Popping him out of my mouth, I prayed that my knees stayed strong as I got on top and lowered myself down onto his thick dick. Eye contact was everything, feeling his hands caressing my hips then ass had me cupping my breast and pinching my nipples. I found my tempo and slowly picked up my pace.

I forgot the advantages of riding dick. I was a minute in doing so and was already feeling the burn in my legs.

"Get on your knees and ride baby, I don't need you struggling with my baby in you. You don't got to over work yourself the pussy is top tier."

I blushed at what he had said, I just didn't want to give up so soon and get on my knees. He sat up a little and started sucking my titties. I could feel his dick growing more harder inside of me as my pussy contracted around his girth. Listening to Nayvius grunt had me flattening my feet on the bed as I imagined myself twerking for him. Placing my hands on my knees, I made my ass jump.

"Got dammit, you showing the fuck out." Showing out wasn't even the saying for what I was doing. I felt sexy and exotic as hell. Nayvius eyes focused on my titties bouncing as his rough hands roamed my ass had me making my pussy sucking on to his dick for dear life. Finally giving in to the burning of my legs, and the pain in my knees, I placed my hands on Nayvius hard chest and got on my knees.

I felt relief, slowing my pace as I rocked back and forth while he feasted and sucked on my nipples.

"You ain't even taking all of this dick like you pose to Jai." He grabbed my hips and thrust upward causing me to gasp and readjust to the added length. My pussy gushed out more for him as we moaned together. I opened my legs wider as Nayvius reached between my thighs to play with my swollen clit.

"Oh babyyyy."

"You like that shit don't you." I nodded my head, feeling myself tear up with satisfaction.

"I love this shit." I cooed enjoying the feel of his rough hands sliding up and down the sides of my stomach. The sounds of my pussy smacking and our heavy breathing could be heard bouncing off the walls right now. The steady pleasure of him thrusting upwards inside of me made me feel like he was making my pussy see stars or the entire fuckin' universe. I started to tremble; my eyes started to roll into the back of my head. A tingly warmth feeling spread throughout my pussy as he continued to strum my clit.

The sensation of my orgasm building inside of me started

to feel like a rubber bad that's getting stretched to its limit, getting ready to pop. Nayvius held me still as he hammered into me with my clit throbbing and my body shaking.

"Baby…" I whined as I bit into my bottom lip hard. "I'm fenna nut too, so cum all over my shit while I feel you up." The stream of tears was flowing, the feeling was overpowering. I felt a deep pressure as an electrical jolt hit my entire body. A dizzy tornado full of sensations consumed me and I couldn't think of anything else right now because it felt like I wouldn't stop cumming.

I collapsed on the side of Nayvius as he pulled me up until I was halfway laying on his chest listening to the sound of his heart beating fast. Before I knew it, I had fallen into a deep sleep.

When I woke back up Nayvius and I showered and ate. It was about four in the evening now. I called and checked up on my kids and was happy to hear them enjoying their time with Rodrik and his girlfriend. Rodrik's new girlfriend reminded me of the young me. When I was just head over heels for him ignoring all the red flags that he had. She seemed sweet and gentle; I didn't completely trust her just yet with my kids, but I felt that she would treat them right. I wasn't a fighter but behind my kids I was willing to do jail time if a person even coughed wrong around them.

"You really love me Nay?" I blinked twice then rubbed his arm enjoying the feeling of us being laid up and caressing one another.

"I love you, Jaiden. Like in love with you that fast. Ain't no time cap on when a person fall in love. I even tried to google that shit to be sure I wasn't tripping." He chuckled lowly, I rolled my eyes and looked up into his eyes. Nayvius always googled some shit, so I believed him.

"Nah on some real shit though, there's no time frame

when it comes to love baby. I knew I was falling in love with you when I felt like I caught a virus or some shit because you just cut a nigga off cold turkey. I'd wake up thinking about you then end up going to sleep thinking about you. Shit had me off track with my day-to-day life because I couldn't get you off my damn mind for the life of me. When I wasn't busy in the streets, a nigga was wondering how your days was going at school or work. I really didn't want to be on no crazy nigga stalker shit like I told you I would be on. Shit, no lie… I wanted to bust down ya door and bring you and the kids back here and make you stop ignoring me. I know you're beautiful and delicate. I don't want you out here living hard, I want all that soft life shit that them bitches on the gram be talking about." We both shared a laugh as he imitated how females be hash tagging soft girl era in their captions.

"I wanted to prove to you and myself that I could go about things differently. With more patience, and self-control. I never had none of that installed in me since a kid, its why I always fucked up and made my parents disappointed with my decision. Anything that I ever wanted I got, half the time I considered that shit to be easy as fuck. Then I found myself at Rodrik's house, I really went there to have a talk with him about me stepping up to the plate with his daughters, but the girls were already there. I could see nothing but you shining bright through them, they looked at me with bright innocent eyes like they needed an extra male figure like me in their lives to protect and guide them. I second guessed myself thinking that I couldn't be that man for the job. Something told me later on that night after I left Rodrik house that I could be that man for the job. I reflected how I adapted automatically playing on the floor with barbie dolls and doing teatime with Jayla while her bitch ass daddy and grandma stand behind me looking pissed." I laughed because I could imagine Rodrik and his bitter momma giving Nayvius the stank face.

"Are you scared Nay? I'll be honest, I'm scared just a little. I keep thinking that we moving too damn fast and now a baby is in the mix."

"Hell yea, I'm scared... Scared of fucking up. I don't want to lose you. It feel too right to be wrong. Then google said when I asked if men fall in love fast that it's true. That shit said that men fall in love pretty fast. That on average, it can take a man a few months or eighty-eight days. Something to do with testosterone or some shit." He got quiet as I sat up and looked at him like he was crazy. Seconds later Nayvius was busting up laughing as I playfully socked him in the chest.

"I'm just playing but then again, I'm not. I was confused man cause Midas kept clowning saying that I fell for your ass, so I had to google some shit to see if my feelings were valid. I know I'm in love with you though like I said on some real shit." He pulled me into him, making sure he grabbed my ass in the process.

"I was in love with all this ass first though, watching that ass jiggle as you walked down the street in them tight ass leggings. Then I saw you through both eyes even my blind eye, them pretty ass eyes were alluring as fuck and you ain't make shit easy for a nigga. You know what the fuck you be doing Jaiden... just don't hurt a nigga." He kissed me on top of my nose.

"Had me licking and eating booty, I ain't never did no shit like that before." He chuckled. The more we talked and joked around the more I found myself feeling like we weren't moving too fast; we were moving at our own destined pace.

MIDAS

 ive Months Later

"Awww shit! Niggga! Y'all got me out here with fuckin' sharks and shit! I got a baby on the way! I can't be risking my life like this!" Diamond and I laughed so hard that my head had started to throb. We were in the middle of the ocean on vacation in Jamaica, trying to catch fish to bring back to our villa for our chef to cook. Nayvius yelled every time he saw a shark, dolphin or anything that looked big swim past our boat. The fisherman looked at Goof with an annoyed facial expression. He was trying to have patience, but I could tell that it was rubbing off.

I walked to the other side of the boat and gazed at the water. The water was pale blue with white sand, looking out at the coral reefs surrounding the island, my eyes lifted up to the sky, I thanked God. I could feel the connection between me and God every day the more I prayed. With each prayer, there was a calm that came over me. It felt like I had been forgiven for all of my sins.

I had been disciplining myself for months now when it came to everything. Stepping away from my illegal side of things had been easy. My son stepped into my shoes with no error. He now dressed the part and walked the walk. Now I was on my first vacation in over a decade just relaxing and enjoying the fruits of what I worked hard for. I had the people that meant something to me around me and the shit felt really good.

"You always look like you in deep thought Pops." I chuckled, turning slightly to look over at Diamond. It took Diamond a while to refer to me as that, but it didn't take long for us to start bonding.

"It's good to have time to yourself just to think son. So always welcome it and then learn how to turn your thoughts off because those thoughts will keep you up all night." I patted his shoulder.

"Yea, I know... I only sleep four hours out the day." He chuckled, we both looked across the way at Goof shouting again, he jumped hard as the fisherman tried to coach him on how to rail the fish in. Instead of Goof listening he threw the fishing rod into the ocean.

"Tell that nigga that he bet not mess up our dinner for the night. The women want fish, and I don't know about y'all women but if my lady wants fish then she is getting just that." I said with a straight face not fucking around. Anything that Aubry wanted she got it from me. Half the time she didn't have to say it because I just assumed and made it happen. Aubry didn't ask for much so whenever she hinted about wanting something or just flat out asked, I provided it for her.

"Princess not my girl Pops. She really like my best friend right now. I just brought her here with me as a gift because

I'm really proud of her. She has been on her shit, and she is back in school." I noticed when he talked about Princess, his smile would reach his eyes.

"You don't got to convince me. I see the way you look at her."

"I got love for her, but us being together ain't in the cards right now. I don't want to get in the middle of her becoming a better woman for herself. I'm just here to support her and be in her corner. That's something she never had in a person besides her best friend Jaiden. I can tell she starting to love herself and discover herself more plus I'm still doing me and I ain't ready to settle down. I like what we have now. A solid friendship, relationships change the dynamics of things." I nodded my head in agreement.

Diamond walked off to go tell Goof what I had said then Goof big, mouth ass went into silly mode talking big shit. My mind went back to my son and Princess being close. I didn't want it but at the same time I didn't care about what they had going on. I just didn't want my son being taken advantage of. He was grown and had to make his own decision making.

My momma was against Princess being around, so Princess stayed away and did things with Diamond while we were out here on vacation. I didn't want her around me either. It was no hard feelings; I just couldn't rock with her or pretend to be cool with her. Aubry was here and I didn't want to put her in an uncomfortable position. Jaiden told her mom all about Princess and put her up on game. Just as I thought, Aubry kept shit classy and even went out with her daughter and Princess when we first got here.

The coincidence was crazy, Aubry being Jaiden's mom and Princess being Jaiden's best friend while I was Princess ex.

"Nigga how the fuck you whipped the way you are and

you ain't even get the pussy yet?" Goof sat on the bench, taking the blunt from behind his ear he sparked it then looked up at me with a silly smirk on his face.

"It's just the Midas touch, me learning and connecting with Aubry on a deeper level other than sex is more important to me." Was all I offered to say. The way I went about things with Aubry was none of their business. I wanted to make love to Aubry's mental first and grasp a deep connection emotionally before it became physical. I had her now emotionally so this trip would start our physical tie together.

I could feel Aubry's frustration, the way she gazed at me. Her eyes were full of need, but I was the king of discipline. I could hold out from sex for a long time because I didn't let my dick control me. The time was perfect now for us to take it there and so that was my plan while we were on vacation. I wanted it perfect for her so she could understand why it was worth the wait.

I didn't want to set the tone of having casual sex with Aubry. I paid close attention to her just to study who she truly was. Aubry was a good ass woman, a hard worker and the type to nurture you. I was a grown man, and I knew what I wanted out of a woman. I also knew that I could multiply whatever she was giving. I wanted someone who was thoughtful, caring, loving and kind. I want her soft, showing her feminine side.

That was my Aubry, she showed that she was trustworthy, faithful even though we hadn't placed any title on us. We went with the flow and enjoyed each other's company. She was also very reliable as an adult; she had her shit together. Now that I had accepted change and took the steps that needed to be taken when it came to the way that I made side money. I was ready to fully step to her with my shit together not putting her in harm's way or leave her to worry what all I was keeping away from her. I was coming to Aubry as an honest hard-working man willing to do whatever to keep that smile on her face and make her happy.

She had it hard growing up and she recognized and accepted accountability for the mistakes and poor decisions that she had made along the way. I couldn't do anything but respect that and fall for her more. I loved how she was always calm and relaxed. Beauty to me was more than make-up and high-end clothes. Aubry was neat and clean; she always smelled like heaven and took pride in herself.

She had me and my mom using all of her handmade oils and body creams that she was now taking more seriously with me pushing her to create her own skin care shop so she could see a profit from it. I got lost in her beauty each time I laid eyes on her. It was just a connection that I never wanted to lose.

She uplifted me with her strength, empathy, wisdom, and compassion. Her great sense of humor made my tough days seem easy.

"Look at your pops, just lovesick and shit." Goof coughed a little on his blunt as we started to head back towards shore.

"Nigga what?" I tilted my head to the side.

"I went to this nigga house a week ago and he answered the door with makeup on and barrettes in his fucking head. Nigga talking bout I'm whipped when he over here doing all kinds of crazy shit."

"That's my fiancé and if my daughters want to use me as a mannequin, so be it." Goof got serious as silence loomed over us. I looked at him and couldn't hold back my laughter. Nigga could always dish out shit talking but mention Jaiden or the kids and all the goofiness attached to him would fall away.

"Love sure looks good on you, my nigga." I took the blunt away from his sensitive ass and toked on it.

"Shit love look good on y'all niggas too. Got me out here catching fish and shit, bout to lose my damn life." Goof complained.

"I don't got the love bug, I just fuck with Princess heavy." Diamond shrugged as me and Goof looked over at each other.

"Nigga please!" We both said in union.

"If you weren't my son then Princess definitely wouldn't be on this damn trip. How I know you love her is even after you know the extent of her you still help her and keep her around. You make sure she's happy and you care about her well-being. Nothing wrong with that shit, by the time you found out everything you know now you already established something with her. That's the main reason why I ain't tripping."

"Yea cause that chick really did a number on ya Pops. Had that nigga-"

"Shut the fuck up Nayvius!" I cut Goof off before his mouthy ass could go into too much detail. Goof threw his hands up in surrender and chuckled.

"I think it's just something about big broads." Goof shook his head and looked out into the ocean like he was in deep thought before he continued.

"I mean, I got my dosage of a big girl and never wanted to go back to the norm. It's just something about them, the way niggas try to down talk on them is crazy as fuck to me. They smell good, be about their shit, treat a nigga like a king. They deserve the fucking world.... Well.... I don't really know about your big girl Nephew... Yours is different is all a nigga gone say." Goof looked over at Diamond and we all fell out laughing. Princess was one of a kind, a cold piece of work.

"Princess good, she been getting on her shit so she can join the good big girl committee." Diamond chuckled.

"The big girl committee?" I raised my brows.

"Hell yea, Midas. It's a big girl committee or community. All I know is extra meat makes the belly full. Jaiden keeps a nigga full in every aspect." We stepped off the boat still talking shit and laughing at the shit that Goof said until we made it to the Villa that I shared with Aubry. Goof stopped me before I turned the doorknob to walk inside. Diamond walked past us and opened the door as me and Goof took a seat on the porch.

"Real shit my nigga, I'm proud of you. I'm proud of us. I got a family and I love that shit. Shit done changed overnight for us. Look at our surroundings. All we ever known was grinding and counting up M's. We never even got to enjoy our shit and really see what all life had to offer outside of the grind. I thank you as well my nigga. You never selfish with moms either. She really means the world to me, and she done picked me up when I was close to falling off bad. You my brother, that's real shit. We don't really express ourselves, but Jaiden been teaching me a lot especially when it comes to being vocal and not holding back because life is short."

I looked over at Goof and couldn't believe how mature and well-grounded he sounded. I was happy for my boy Jaiden was what he needed in his life. That shit changed him for the better. He was even more calm and all he talked about was Jaiden and the kids. Goof had started his construction company and kept himself busy and out of the streets. I worried a little thinking that it would be harder for him to leave the drug shit alone because he had adapted to hustling at a very young age.

There is a big difference with hustling because you have to and hustling because it gave an adrenaline rush. The need for more was always there, which made it harder to walk away.

"My nigga, I'm proud of you in so many ways. I worried when you lost your parents because I saw a shift in you. You no longer had shit to live for, so you went harder like you were invincible or like you welcomed the possibility of death. Now you have a beautiful family. They are the center of your universe like it should be. I always got you and your family and I'm here for you anytime my nigga." I stood up as we slapped hands and embraced each other like real brothers.

"You know what I told Jaiden this morning?" Goof looked serious like he was about to say something important.

"What you tell her?"

"I said... I was excited... cause I was falling, falling in love with her... Now that I've falling what am I gonna dooooooo!" He sang loud and clear, and I couldn't do shit but just drop my head and laugh. As he continued his bullshit ass singing.

"I'll do whatever puts a smile on my baby's face... Jaiden's my best friend!!!! And she could never be replaced." I said fuck it and got goofy with him, singing Tyrese "Falling in Love" song. Clearing my throat, I threw my head back as Goof snapped his fingers and stomped his feet. I couldn't really sing but I had a little something in me.

"Here and my life, just her and I... We can go anywhere we want to! I'm living my life with her by my side. Aye, one day I'ma make her my wife, yes, I am!" Goof two-stepped and sung the chorus as I continued the ad-libs. This was what real love turned us into. Some sappy ass, love-sick niggas.

I looked through the villa's window and laid eyes on Aubry. She didn't look a day over twenty-five. The women sat around in the living room listening to whatever my mom was saying. Aubry had honey blonde braids to compliment her smooth caramel complexion. Her chinky eyes tightened as she smiled at whatever Jaiden had said. My eyes roamed her face, loving the way her dimples were on display, her smile reaching her eyes as she threw her head back to laugh.

Aubry rocked a Jamaican knitted dress with her milky thick thighs out on display. Licking my lips, I grunted thinking about the self-discipline I had when it came to making love to her. That discipline was wearing off, I just hoped she was ready to release it all to me. Once I entered her, her soul would tie into mine and stay knotted together forever.

AUBRY

"I don't know why I let y'all convince me to come to Jamaica." Ms. Wellington took a small sip of whatever was in her cup. I was ready to get up and smell whatever it was because her words were starting to slur. She knew better than to be drinking anything. She healed eighty percent, but indulging in alcohol wouldn't mix well with the medication that she still had to take.

"As your doctor…" I started but was cut off by Ms. Wellington sitting up sluggishly pointing in my direction. Yea, she's definitely tipsy. I thought to myself shaking my head.

"As my daughter-in-law I ain't tryna hear all that medical kind of talk. I only really came to see all the lovey-dovey stuff because soon I'll have even more grandkids to brag about." She readjusted herself and looked over at me and Jaiden smiling. I loved Ms. Wellington. She was stubborn but was kind-hearted and sweet. She spoiled my grandkids and accepted Jaiden with no problem as her own. It's like we had a big family that was full of good love. I kind of wished Cherry was here so we could build our friendship back up, but she offered to stay back with the kids to let Jaiden get a break.

Me spending majority of my years lonely with no one to turn to after my husband died had me more grateful now than ever. My only regret was holding back too long and not revealing myself to Jaiden sooner.

"Ma you need anything?" Diamond walked inside of the villa looking just like his father. Diamond and Midas' bond was growing by the day. He took to Ms. Wellington and spent nights at her house keeping an eye on her whenever me and Midas were busy. I still worked at the hospital but now I was doing that part-time. I enjoyed creating and helping Midas add things to his university that could benefit the students and staff.

I fell in love with Midas, deeply in love. He was patient and it was just something about his touch that had me sprung off of him like we were high school lovers.

We were still dating, he'd pick me up, take me out on dates, send flowers to my house, and lunch when I was at work. He was very thoughtful, and I appreciated him taking things slow with me. I grew super close with Jaiden and my grandbabies, so my free time I split between them and Midas.

"I need for you to go get me some more of that cranberry juice out of the kitchen with ice baby." She smiled at him innocently.

"Ms. Wellington-" I was cut off by Midas walking in with Nayvius following behind him. Midas, Midas, Midas…. He was so damn fine and captivating that I couldn't help myself gazing at him like he was the entire entree. We still hadn't had sex and that was starting to become frustrating. I wondered what was up with that, but I didn't want to seem thirsty. I was enjoying us just being intimate, constantly peeling back layers of each other in the most authentic way.

We always came close to doing it, but it would never go all the way. Midas would come over to my house, get me naked, massage and oil my body down from head to toe, while he asked all about my day. When he was finished, he'd hold me until I was snoring like a baby. He planned this entire trip to celebrate his mom's healing and finishing all of her physical therapy sessions. He also mentioned how he was proud of him and Nayvius and felt like they should celebrate their major moves and steps they took to change for the better.

"You good baby?" I looked up into his eyes and squeezed my thighs tight. Right now, it felt like it was only him and I in the room. My eyes dropped down to his chest then his abs, I tried to keep my eyes from dropping down to his dick print in the swim trunks he had on, it was just impossible to ignore.

"Aubry?" His deep voice felt like he had penetrated me. Licking my lips and just gazing into his eyes had me feeling like I was slow.

"Umm yea, I'm good did you guys catch the fish?" I asked smiling, Midas looked at me like he knew what I was thinking and nodded his head.

"Naw man, Midas caught a couple, I wasn't risking my life with all them damn sharks." Nayvius cut in.

"Sharks? It wasn't no sharks, them was just big ass fish." Midas corrected him.

"Them was sharks' man!" Nayvius protested just as Diamond walked back in with Ms. Wellington.

"I think you need to see what your mom is over there sipping on." I tried to whisper lowly making sure that she didn't hear me telling on her.

"Alright, I'll see y'all tomorrow. Princess and I are going

to Nine Mile today." Diamond leaned down to kiss Ms. Wellington on the forehead.

"You just be careful with that girl, she had us all fooled, but I believe in second chances, and I trust that your judgment is good." Ms. Wellington eyed Diamond like she was worried. I personally didn't know Princess like that, but Midas told me all about her. My daughter also told me how she felt like Princess was just surrounded by people that never really cared about her.

I didn't feel any kind of way with her being here on this trip because she was before me concerning Midas. I just thought it was weird that she was now openly messing with Midas' son which made me feel like that's the best she could do since she couldn't have Midas anymore. I just prayed that she didn't hurt Diamond like she did Midas because Diamond was a good kid in my eyes. Princess was a little too old for him but at the same time, age really didn't matter when you were grown and able to make your own decisions.

"I got something special for you planned tonight." Midas squatted until he was eye level with me. His rough hands rubbed up and down my soft thighs, making me quiver inside from his magical touch. He watched me intently as I watched him, Midas didn't talk as much but when he did it always meant something. When he felt relaxed and well rested, he really expressed himself.

I noted that Midas was a good observer. He always sat quietly and listened as everyone talked and at the end of the conversation, he would throw in his two cents. His eyes were dreamy and captivating, a burning sensation of anticipation grew inside of me wondering what exactly he had planned. I just loved being in his space, close and intimate with him.

"You just gotta stay here for a little while longer so I can set things up for you. Tonight, we solidify our union. So, while you wait, I want you to really think about if you're ready to spend the rest of your life with me." I nodded my head slowly as he leaned in close to kiss me on the lips.

"I know I do." I stated honestly.

"Good, set your alarm. Walk over to our villa in about an hour in twenty." A warmth spread throughout my chest. Before he stood up, he kissed me again, this time he sucked my bottom lip then nibbled on it. I sighed and tried to keep it together in a room full of onlookers. Midas stood to his feet and walked over to his mom, took the cup out of her hand, then brought the cup to his full set of lips and started gulping down whatever was in the cup.

"No more rum punch and I mean it Ma. You know that Aubry instructed you to only drink wine here and there. Besides, rum punch don't ever taste right with cranberry juice." Midas frowned as he got on his mom's case. She folded her arms in front of her chest fake pouting. Which looked so cute.

The men ended up leaving, once Midas end up making his mom go to her room to rest. Some days she was drowsy due to the different medications that she had to take. I stayed back and chilled with Jaiden for a while trying to make time pass. I was too excited to see what Midas had in store.

He was so romantic and thoughtful. Each date we went on he planned, and I always ended up liking what we would end up doing.

"You love him huh mom?" I looked over at Jaiden and blushed, the corners of my lips turned upwards as I thought about the kind of man Midas was. He was the type that deserved to be catered too. I wanted him to feel like I treated him like a king because he made me feel like a queen twenty-four seven.

"I do, I mean it makes me question what me and Alex

had. I try not to compare it because there really is no comparison, but it does make me wonder and question myself and my past marriage. Alex was a good man, but Midas is extraordinary. I know this is TMI, but we haven't had sex and I feel so physically connected to him. Emotionally it's everything to me. After my mom was killed, I had this anxious attachment thing going on with myself where I use to fear being abandoned. I know my mom didn't plan on getting killed but as the only child, I felt that way. When Alex use to leave to go to work that same anxious feeling would be there. It's crazy because I knew that one day, he would end up leaving me, I just didn't know when or how. With Midas, I know that life isn't promised but I can feel that he is my soul mate."

Jaiden teared up a bit, rubbing her cute baby bump.

"I feel that with Nay as well. The way he love and adore me feels so unreal. I guess that's why you didn't treat Princess a way when we all hung out. Midas makes you feel secure and even though you haven't had sex with him, you have the confidence and trust to believe that he really has no feelings for Princess anymore."

"Your right, also our bond is really deep Jai. I can be my true self and open up to Midas. He shows me genuine interest in everything I say or do. It's the top tier respect for me that he shows and how special he makes me feel. We are there for each other emotionally and physically. We feed each other spiritual food to have the presence of God between us. Honestly, I feel like its true love because of the absolute affection, devotion fondness and the warmth that hits me all over every time we are around each other."

"That's really deep. I feel that with my Nay as well. Makes me feel like Rodrik ass was just a place holder." We both shared a giggle as I checked my phone to see how much time had gone by.

"Well, I think it's time for me to see what Midas, has in store for me." We both fell out laughing again as I stood to my feet stretching.

"I'll see you tomorrow for our massages on the logs." Jaiden pouted.

"Nayvius is coming with us, he said can't no nigga out here massage on me and touch my body. Nay said he's going to do the massage and ask them for the white stuff that they be putting on the women bodies."

"At least he's offering the massage." I giggled.

"Yea I can't fault him for that. He said he googled what kind of women Jamaican men like... They love big girls. That man uses google for everything." I liked Nayvius he was really funny, anytime we all were together, he constantly made everyone laugh. He and Jaiden were deeply in love, one look at them as a couple and you could feel the potent love swarming between the two of them. That was good for my god-kids as well. I helped Jaiden stand to her feet as we walked out of the villa together.

The scenery here snatched my breath away each time I walked outside. Our villas were kind of close together with the ocean a couple feet away. Jaiden and my villa were right next together. We both instantly teared up and looked at each other as we gazed at the trail of roses leading up to both of our villas. I turned to look at Jaiden as I embraced my daughter tight.

"One thing for sure, is we got some men that really love us. I'm pretty sure the night will be interesting for the both of us. Enjoy baby." I winked at her and started to follow the trail of roses. These villas that we were staying in weren't just regular. They were extravagant and big, so big that we all could have just lived in one together.

Opening the door, roses were everywhere, making me wonder just how Midas pulled all of this off and in such a short time. I gazed at the foyer entrance which was beautiful. There were roses on the chandelier and along the sweeping staircase. Small candles were also lit creating a nice path for me to follow. Wiping at my tear-stricken face. I swallowed down hard trying to fight back my emotions.

There was so much thought put into what Midas had done for me in this very moment. Walking up the steps slowly, I could hear Tyrese "What Am I Gonna Do." Song playing lowly from our room that was all the way down the hall on the second floor. My hands got clammy as I reached for the door handle to open up the door.

Midas sat with nothing, but a towel wrapped around his waist. Seeing him sitting there looking handsome as hell with his deep set of eyes penetrating me made my body tingle from head to toe.

"Get naked." His deep baritone voice made my body ache with longing for him. I lifted the knitted dress above my head, then removed my panties, just as Midas stood up to approach me. I wasn't ashamed of my curvaceous body, but it made me wonder if the natural sag of my breast would bother Midas. My breasts weren't perky and sitting up at attention, but they were full and natural.

Midas took away any second guessing at the moment. His eyes were filled to the brim with lust. Latching onto my left nipple with his mouth, he cupped both of my breasts and massaged them as he took turns with both nipples, licking and sucking with the right amount of pressure. Tossing my head back and moaning, I could feel my pussy leaking and yearning to be filled with all of him.

I couldn't go another night with foreplay, I had to have all of Midas today.

"Let me take care of you." He released my breast and grabbed my hand. When he turned to walk away and guide the way for both of us, I stood still, making him turn around to face me with confusion.

Licking my lips, I knew that this was going to sound too blunt and to the point, but I had to make it clear exactly what it was that I wanted. A closed mouth would starve and for the past couple of months, Midas had me starving.

"Your touch is amazing Midas. I fell in love with just your touch first. Then it was followed up by your actions and the way you treat me and carry yourself as a mature grown man."

"What you trying to say baby?" My body started to quiver with a strong desire that I hadn't felt in a long time.

"I'm trying to say in the nicest way possible, that I umm... I want some dick Midas." Silence took over as we stared into each other's eyes deeply. Midas rubbed his chin hair and dropped his head low. My stomach tightened; my nerves were officially ruined right now as I felt ungrateful for all he had done to set the mood for another one of his romantic nights.

"That's what I'm trying to give you. I wasn't going to make you wait any longer...Let me clean you and massage you, then you can have all the dick you want." He licked his lips, as I stood there speechless. Gesturing his hand for me to walk in front of him, I took timid steps ahead of him then jumped at his hand colliding with my ass. The flood between my legs started to seep from between my southern lips as I kept walking to the ensuite bathroom.

The bathroom reminded me of a spa inspired bathroom. It had a super deep garden tub, a walk-in rain shower and underfloor heating, warming the soles of my feet with each step I took. Natural stones, mosaic tiles and high-quality fixtures evoked a sense of tranquility making it feel like heaven on earth. I noticed that a bubble bath was already run for me with roses floating on top. Before I could lift my foot to step into the tub, Midas had come up behind me, making me bend all the way down until my hands were touching my toes.

"That pussy already wet from my touch alone. You want this dick just as bad as I've been wanting this pussy. You on birth control." I could feel his thick head teasing the opening to my sopping wet center.

"Noooo." I moaned out just as he gripped my hips and thrusted all the way inside of me.

"Good baby, everything from this moment forward is going to go pretty fast. Remember this date and time. It's for sure the date of conception of our baby. I'm going to fuck this pussy up, I'ma go hard, and pound the bottom of it out, then go soft making sure to hit all the spots that you probably never knew existed inside of you." Breath baited; my walls collapsed around his thick dick. I struggled with catching my breath as my eyes shut tightly.

My pussy savored the feeling of his length stuffed deep inside of me. Midas' grip on my waist tightened as he started to pull all the way out, only to push all the way back in making me gasp out for air. His hands drifted to my collarbone as he continued thrusting in and out of me powerfully. I was never big on moaning during sex but with the way Midas was fucking me had me moaning and pleading like I was begging for life.

His hands were all over me, every muscle in my body tensed from anticipation. Gliding his large hands down the middle of my breast until he was cupping and pinching my breast had me losing my balance. When I felt myself falling his hand went right under my stomach. Holding me up as he never missed a beat inside of me stroking.

"You wanted this dick." He lifted his foot and placed it on the garden tub. Suddenly it felt like him lifting his foot gave him more leverage. His dick felt like it was going way deeper then where it was supposed to go. The moans were now silenced, my whole world felt like it stopped and started rotating and spinning around Midas.

I couldn't move, couldn't breathe, my body started to spasm.

"You gotta take all this dick baby. I gotta fuck some patience into you and punish this pussy because you messed up my smooth plans for the night." The sensation of his dick had turned me into clay. It felt like Midas owned every single inch of me and I had surrendered my soul, body, and mind right over to him with each fucking stroke he delivered.

Heat swirled throughout my entire body as my breast moved back and forth with heaviness. He reached between my legs and strummed my sensitive bud until I started to spasm, my knees buckled but once again, Midas held me upward securing me in his arms. He still kept stroking through my intense orgasm that had me seeing tiny silver stars.

Midas spun me around until my breasts were pressed up against his chest. Without saying anything, he picked me up and carried me out of the bathroom.

"I guess we getting filthy before we get clean." He carried me to the round king size bed laying me down gently.

With no shame, I opened my legs wide, knees apart. Playing in my wetness as Midas got on the bed to fall between my legs. He picked my foot up and placed it onto his shoulder then entered me slowly. I sat up a little with a deep arch in my back as he pushed me backwards making me lay back down.

"Relax baby." Moving in and out of me, my entire body came alive as I bucked a little from the intense orgasm, I had seconds ago. Closing my eyes for only a few seconds, my eyes popped right back open at the cool feeling of Midas mouth sucking my toes. His tongue flickered between each toe as he glided with ease inside of me, stretching my walls out to its capacity.

Midas was strumming my body like it was his favorite instrument. I now understood what took him so long to give me this feeling. It was all about patience, I never expected this to be over-the-top mind-blowing. I didn't even feel like myself, no I felt like Midas's woman. The only woman for him, I already was staking my claim. This wasn't an ordinary feel-good dick or sex session. This was the *I'm with all the bullshit, ready to die bout this dick,* type of feeling.

"You made my self-control evaporate, Aubry. I was going to wait until I placed that half-a-million-dollar ring on your finger." I figured Midas was just talking sex talk. So, I moaned and sniffled trying my best to keep up with each stroke he delivered.

"Babyyy... I'm about to-"

"Hold that for me baby, control yourself. Don't cum yet for me, wait until I'm lapping that pussy up with my tongue." His husky deep voice alone had me ready to explode. My feet clenched up as I tried to steady my breathing and hold back from cumming all over him.

He slid out of me, and I wanted to pull my hair out and beg him to put it back in.

"I want you on top." I blinked my eyes as I watched him lay flat on his back. My anxiety rose high as I started thinking too deep into it. Riding? My knees are not how they used to be, but in this moment, I wanted to please Midas like he had pleased me. I just didn't want to let him down, but I also didn't want to feel the pain in my knees from trying to pop it on him like I was Megan Thee Stallion.

"On top of my face baby, now. You ain't gotta do too much just let me eat that pussy thoroughly." I ran my fingertips over his sculpted upper body until they ran over his bulging six-pack. Midas' veins running down his biceps and forearms. He was in good shape, and it made him look even more sexy. I licked my lips as I timidly tried to situate myself so that my pussy was lined up perfectly with his picture-perfect handsome face.

I gasped hard when he dragged his hot tongue up my pulsating slit. Midas' teeth started to graze my pussy as I tried to control the way I bucked onto his face from the pleasurable sensation his tongue produced. Staring intensely into my eyes, he thrusted his tongue between my fat pussy lips making me shake hard. Next, it felt like Midas was literally French kissing and making out with my pussy nastily.

My eyes watered from the feeling as I leaned a little forward to clutch some of his short coils. Not once did he blink his eyes as he kept his focus on me, kissing, licking, and sucking my pussy like he needed it to survive. Heat spiraled throughout me as my eyes started to roll back into my head. This feeling was out of this world, every rational thought fled my brain as I struggled to even moan.

He took his tongue out of my sticky center and sucked on my clit with the right amount of pressure. It hadn't even been two full minutes and an orgasm was taking over my entire body, ceasing me still until I violently shook. Midas didn't stop and my body had a mind of its own. I felt a little embarrassed because I knew it looked like I was possessed by a damn sex demon.

My eyes felt like they were getting stuck into the back of my head as I bit into my bottom lip until I tasted blood. I tried to look down to make sure I was suffocating Midas, each time I looked into his eyes it was just too much. Midas gave me a knowing look like he knew he was possessing and claiming me as his.

"Oh baby, I don't think I can take anymore." He released my clit and smirked.

"But you can, Aubry. You got more pent-up frustration in you, and I need it all in my mouth." He drove his tongue into me, then massaged my swollen clit with the pad of his thumb. Midas was ripping me apart; my thoughts were jumble and my body tingled all over. His tongue sank deeper inside of me as the arch in my back curved like the crescent moon.

I moaned so loud it sounded like I was screaming. I tried to get off of his face, but he pulled me back down by holding my waist. It was so much pleasure mixed with a little bit of pain each time his teeth grazed my pussy on purpose. So much pleasure that it felt like he could snatch all the wind and breath out of me. It felt like I was about to die and go to heaven as the happiest woman on earth.

I was so wet and turned on for Midas that I could see my essence painted all over his nose and cheeks.

"Please baby." Whap! He slapped me on my left butt cheek making it ripple as he moved his face up and down then side to side making a bigger mess on his face. I could feel another climax taking over me and this time every muscle in my body seized as I started to sob out crying. He wasn't rendering any kind of mercy. I got desperate to chase my next orgasm as a weird warm sensation took over me making me feel like I was floating outside in the pale blue sea.

I rocked back and forth on his face while his rough hands

probably left marks from smacking each ass cheek from left to right. Dipping his thick tongue deep inside of me while his nose added the right amount of pressure to my clit had me screaming and falling backwards but Midas sat up and followed me until I was on my back bucking and shaking as liquid squirted out of me onto his face. He lapped up every single drop leaving me panting and wondering just where the hell did my soul go.

Midas placed gentle pecks between my sticky thighs and got off the bed with an unfazed look plastered on his face. I knew right then that I had to redeem myself the next round but right now, my body was still spasming and sleep was fighting to take over.

"I got the Midas Touch baby, giving you the idis like you had a full fucking meal. I'm giving you twenty minutes to get yourself together. I'm just getting warmed up. I got you this big ass villa for a reason so you could rest up and soak that pretty pussy. It's now officially all mine, when I'm done taking care of it you won't walk right for a week straight." He walked off towards the bathroom I assumed.

I was in and out of consciousness when Midas walked back into the room with a hot washcloth. He kissed me on the lips and sleep overtook me.

I woke up still riding a wave that I had never experienced. Midas sat up with his back against the headboard with a small blue box resting in his lap. Without looking at me he spoke.

"I always brag about me having the Midas Touch... My father used to say that us Wellington men had the ability to make everything that we are involved with very successful. We could make everything we touched turn into gold. In some cases that was very true but with my love life, I always came up short handed. It wasn't until I walked into your class reeking of that theory with confidence so potent that I just knew I would have you exactly where I wanted you. I guess you showed me that you had the same kind of touch and ever since you touched me, looked at me and opened your mouth to bless me with your words. I've felt stuck in love and wanting more and more of you. To knock down those tall ass walls that you keep in place to protect you and the trauma that you have been through. I don't got to wonder if this will be successful or not because I believe in it, I know this was meant to be and I want it forever. I don't want to leave this island with us going to separate homes and living separate lives. These past couple of months I've changed and maintained my self-discipline to peel back more layers to you to ensure that what we had was worth the sacrifice. When we leave this island, I hope we both leave with the same last name." He stood up and walked over to my side of the bed with the blue box in his hand.

When he stood in front of me, his emotions flitted across his face and so did mine. I brushed the palms of my hands nervously looking up into Midas eyes as he dropped down to one knees making my heartbeat wildly.

"Will you marry me, Aubry?" Even now he reeked of confidence like he knew what my answer would be. I smiled through my tears and nodded my head yes before verbalizing it.

"Yes, I will marry you Midas." He got off his knee and crashed his lips into mine making me fall back onto the bed as he parted my thighs. Sliding into me slowly, I held onto his back as I shut my eyes imagining the rest of my life with Midas.

THE END!!!!!!!!!!!!!!

. . .

PLEASE LEAVE A REVIEW!!!

SUBSCRIBE TO MASTERPIECE

CHECK OUT MY WEBSITE HTTP://WWW.AUTHORESSMAS
TERPIECE.COM

Are you interested in keeping up with more of my releases? To be notified first of all my upcoming releases and sneak peeks, please subscribe to my mailing list! https://bit.ly/3AYIwMK

Contact me on any of my social media handles as well!

Facebook- Authoress Masterpiece & Masterpiece Reads

Facebook private group for updates- Masterpiece Readers

Instagram- authoress_masterpiece & masterpiece_lgee

Email – masterpiece3541@outlook.com

Made in the USA
Columbia, SC
27 July 2024

38873811R00107